AS YOU LIKE IT
SHAKESPEARE FOR KIDS

JEANETTE VIGON

WHY I WROTE THIS BOOK THE WAY I DID

When I embarked on the journey of adapting Shakespeare's plays for children, my primary goal was to bridge the gap between the timeless allure of Shakespeare's narratives and the imaginative worlds of young readers. The decision to adapt these plays for children was driven by a desire to introduce them to the richness of literary classics at an early age, fostering a love for literature that could grow with them.

Choosing to maintain the original structure of acts and scenes was a deliberate effort to preserve the integrity and rhythm of Shakespeare's works. This approach not only honors the original compositions but also introduces young readers to the conventions of drama and the beauty of structured storytelling. It was important to me that children experience the plays as they were intended, albeit in a more accessible form.

Incorporating literary language while ensuring it remains engaging and understandable for children was a balancing act. I aimed to simplify the complexity of Shakespeare's language without diluting its power and beauty. By carefully selecting vocabulary and crafting sentences that convey the essence of the original plays, I aspired to captivate young minds and stimulate their intellectual curiosity.

Adapting these plays also involved making thoughtful choices about content, ensuring that themes and scenes were appropriate for a young audience. This required a sensitive approach to storytelling, where the lessons of love, loyalty, betrayal, and justice are presented in a manner that is both educational and entertaining.

In summary, the creation of this book was a labor of love, guided by the belief that Shakespeare's works are not just for adults but for everyone. By adapting these plays for children, I hope to plant the seeds of appreciation for classic literature in the fertile ground of young imaginations, encouraging a lifelong journey of reading, learning, and discovery.

I truly hope you will enjoy reading it, as much as I enjoyed re-writing it.

INTRODUCTION

Step into the whimsical and somewhat bewildering realm of "As You Like It," where we transport you to the magical Forest of Arden, a place where characters discover themselves and love in its many forms. This isn't merely an ancient narrative about romance and escaping the harsh realities of court life; it's an expedition of self-discovery, freedom, and the extraordinary power of nature to heal and transform.

Our tale unfolds in an era when letters were sealed with wax, not clicked with a send button, and where finding oneself often meant wandering through lush, verdant woods, not scrolling through web pages. Amid the natural beauty of Arden, we find our diverse cast of characters, each fleeing from the constraints and injustices of their former lives, seeking solace and freedom in the forest's embrace.

In one scene, there's Rosalind, the intelligent and spirited daughter of a banished duke, who adopts the guise of a young man, finding liberty and love in her playful deception. Nearby, Orlando, a young gentleman wronged by his brother, discovers his true strength and affections amidst the trees and trials of Arden. And let's not forget the array of characters they meet: jesters, shepherds, and nobles alike, all intertwining in a dance of disguise, desire, and discovery.

But fear not, this tale isn't a somber stroll through the woods —far from it! We're infusing this adventure with laughter, witty banter, and the occasional dose of folly and confusion. Expect to chuckle at mistaken identities, sigh at poetic declarations of love, and maybe even shake your head at the follies of those caught in Cupid's crossfire.

So, find your most comfortable spot and let yourself be enveloped by the enchanting world of "As You Like It." Prepare for a journey where battles of wit replace sword fights, heartfelt verses take the place of solemn speeches, and a story unfolds that teaches us about the liberating power of love and the joy of finding oneself and others in the least expected places.

Are you ready? Then join Rosalind, Orlando, and the entire cast as we step into a narrative cherished for generations, now reimagined with a charm and vibrancy just for you. Off we go into the heart of Arden, where every path leads to discovery, laughter, and, above all, love.

ACT 1

SCENE I

Orlando and Adam walked in the orchard of Oliver's house. The air in the orchard smelled of ripe apples.

Orlando said, "Adam, as I remember, Father left me only one thousand crowns. He told my brother, with his blessing, to raise me well. And that is where my sadness starts. My brother Jaques is at school. People say good things about how much he learns. But he keeps me at home like a country boy. Or more truly, he keeps me here uncared for. Is this how a gentleman should be kept? It is no different from keeping an ox in a shed. His horses are treated better. They are well fed and taught to behave. Riders are hired to train them. But I, his brother, get nothing from him but growing taller. His farm animals get as much. Besides this nothing he gives me, he also takes away my natural good qualities. He makes me eat with his servants. He does not treat me like a brother. He ruins my good manners by not teaching me. This is what makes me sad, Adam. The spirit of my father in me wants to rebel. I will not stand it any longer. But I do not know how to escape it."

Adam said, "There comes my master, your brother."

Orlando told Adam, "Step aside, Adam. You will hear how he will scold me."

Oliver entered the orchard.

Oliver asked, "Now, sir! What are you doing here?"

Orlando replied, "Nothing. I am not taught to make anything."

Oliver asked, "What are you spoiling then, sir?"

Orlando said, "Indeed, sir, I am helping you spoil what God made. I am your poor, unworthy brother, made idle by you."

Oliver said, "Indeed, sir, find better work, and be gone for a while."

Orlando asked, "Shall I keep your pigs and eat husks with them? What large share of money have I wasted to be so poor?"

Oliver asked, "Do you know where you are, sir?"

Orlando replied, "Oh, sir, very well. Here in your orchard."

Oliver asked, "Do you know who you are speaking to, sir?"

Orlando said, "Yes, better than he knows me. I know you are my oldest brother. And as family, you should know me too. The rules of countries say you are better because you are first-born. But that does not take away my family connection. Even if there were twenty brothers between us. I have as much of my father in me as you. Though, I admit, you being older is closer to his memory."

Oliver exclaimed, "What, boy!" Oliver was as cross as a badger woken from a nap.

Orlando said, "Come, come, older brother, you are too young in this argument."

Oliver asked, "Will you put your hands on me, bad person?"

Orlando replied, "I am no bad person. I am the youngest son of Sir Rowland de Boys. He was my father. Anyone who says such a father had bad sons is a bad person three times over. If you were not my brother, I would not take this hand from your throat. Not until my other hand had pulled out your tongue for saying so. You have insulted yourself."

Adam pleaded, "Sweet masters, be patient. For your father's memory, please agree."

Oliver said, "Let me go, I say."

Orlando stated, "I will not, until I am ready. You shall hear me. My father told you in his will to give me a good education. You have trained me like a farm worker. You have hidden all gentleman-like qualities from me. The spirit of my father grows strong in me. I will not stand it any longer. So, let me do things a gentleman does. Or give me the small share my father left me. With that, I will go find my own fortune."

Oliver asked, "And what will you do? Beg, when that is spent? Well, sir, get inside. I will not be troubled with you for long. You shall have some of what you want. Please, leave me."

Orlando said, "I will not bother you more than is good for me."

Oliver told Adam, "Get going with him, you old dog."

Adam asked, "Is 'old dog' my reward? It is true, I have lost my teeth in your service. God be with my old master! He would not have spoken such a word."

Orlando and Adam left.

Oliver said to himself, "Is it so? Are you starting to challenge me? I will cure your rudeness. And I will not give you a thousand crowns either. Hello, Dennis!"

Dennis entered.

Dennis asked, "Did your worship call?"

Oliver asked, "Was not Charles, the duke's wrestler, here to speak with me?"

Dennis replied, "If you please, he is here at the door. He begs to see you."

Oliver said, "Call him in."

Dennis left.

Oliver thought, "This will be a good way. And tomorrow is the wrestling."

Charles entered.

Charles said, "Good morning to your worship."

Oliver greeted him. "Good Monsieur Charles, what is the new news at the new court?"

Charles replied, "There is no news at the court, sir, but the old news. The old duke is banished by his younger brother, the new duke. Three or four loving lords have chosen to leave with him. Their lands and money make the new duke richer. So he lets them wander."

Oliver asked, "Can you tell if Rosalind, the duke's daughter, is banished with her father?"

Charles answered, "Oh, no. For the new duke's daughter, her cousin, loves her so much. They grew up together from when they were babies. She would have followed her into exile, or become very sad to stay behind. She is at the court. Her uncle loves her as much as his own daughter. And never two ladies loved each other as they do."

Oliver asked, "Where will the old duke live?"

Charles said, "They say he is already in the forest of Arden. Many merry men are with him. There they live like the old Robin Hood of England. They say many young gentlemen go to him every day. They pass the time without worries, as in old happy times."

Oliver asked, "What, you wrestle tomorrow before the new duke?"

Charles replied, "Indeed, I do, sir. I came to tell you something. I have been secretly told that your younger brother Orlando plans to enter in a costume. He wants to try a fall against me. Tomorrow, sir, I wrestle for my good name. Anyone who escapes me without a broken bone will do very well. Your brother is young and not strong. For your sake, I would be unwilling to beat him. But I must, for my own honor, if he comes. So, out of my love for you, I came to tell you. Either you can stop him from his plan, or accept the shame he will face. It is his own choice and completely against my will."

Oliver said, "Charles, I thank you for your love to me. You will find I will repay it kindly. I knew of my brother's plan. I have secretly tried to talk him out of it, but he is determined. I will tell you, Charles, he is the most stubborn young fellow in France. He is full of ambition. He is a jealous copier of every man's good skills. He is a secret and bad plotter against me, his own brother. So, use your judgment. I would rather you hurt him badly than just his finger. And you had best be careful. If you shame him even a little, or if he does not look good against you, he will try to poison you. He will trap you with some sneaky trick. He will never leave you until he has taken your life by some indirect means. For I promise you, and I almost speak it with tears, there is no one so young and so bad alive today. I speak only as his brother. But if I described him to you as he truly is, I would blush and weep. And you would look pale and wonder."

Charles said, "I am very glad I came here to you. If he comes tomorrow, I will give him his payment. If he ever walks alone again, I will never wrestle for a prize anymore. And so, God keep your worship!"

Oliver said, "Farewell, good Charles."

Charles left.

Oliver thought, "Now I will encourage this adventurer. I hope I shall see an end of him. For my soul, though I do not know why, hates nothing more than him. Yet he is gentle. He was never schooled and yet is learned. He is full of noble ideas. He is loved by all sorts of people. Indeed, he is so much in the heart of the world. Especially of my own people, who know him best. Because of this, I am not valued at all. But it shall not be so long. This wrestler shall clear all. Nothing remains but that I encourage the boy to go there. Which now I will go about."

Oliver left.

SCENE 2

Celia and Rosalind were on the lawn before the Duke's palace.

Celia said, "Please, Rosalind, my sweet cousin, be merry."

Rosalind replied, "Dear Celia, I show more happiness than I feel. Would you want me to be even merrier? Unless you could teach me to forget a banished father. You must not teach me how to remember any special pleasure."

Celia said, "In this, I see you do not love me as much as I love you. If my uncle, your banished father, had banished your uncle, the duke my father, and you were still with me, I could have taught my love to take your father for mine. So would you, if your love for me were as true as mine is for you."

Rosalind said, "Well, I will forget my own situation, to be happy in yours."

Celia said, "You know my father has no child but me. Nor is he likely to have any. And truly, when he passes away, you shall be his heir. For what he has taken from your father by force, I will give back to you in love. By my honor, I will. And when I break that promise, let me turn into a monster. Therefore, my sweet Rose, my dear Rose, be merry."

Rosalind replied, "From now on I will, cousin, and think of games. Let me see; what do you think of falling in love?"

Celia said, "Indeed, please do, to make a game of it. But do not love any man seriously. Nor play at it more than you can honorably stop with only a slight blush."

Rosalind asked, "What shall be our game, then?"

Celia suggested, "Let us sit and make fun of good lady Fortune from her wheel. So that her gifts may be given out equally from now on." The birds in the palace garden sang sweetly.

Rosalind said, "I wish we could do so. For her benefits are very misplaced. And the generous blind woman makes most mistakes in her gifts to women."

Celia agreed, "'Tis true. For those she makes pretty, she

seldom makes honest. And those she makes honest, she makes very plain-looking."

Rosalind said, "No, now you go from Fortune's job to Nature's. Fortune rules in gifts of the world, not in features given by Nature."

Touchstone, the jester, entered. Touchstone's jokes were as jumbled as a pile of toys.

Celia asked, "No? When Nature has made a pretty creature, may she not by Fortune fall into trouble? Though Nature has given us wit to mock Fortune, has not Fortune sent in this fool to cut off the argument?"

Rosalind said, "Indeed, Fortune is too hard for Nature there. When Fortune makes Nature's fool the one to stop Nature's wit."

Celia said, "Perhaps this is not Fortune's work either, but Nature's. Nature sees our natural wits are too dull to discuss such goddesses. And she has sent this fool as our sharpener. For always the dullness of the fool is the sharpener of the wits. How now, wit! Where are you wandering?"

Touchstone said, "Mistress, you must come away to your father."

Celia asked, "Were you made the messenger?"

Touchstone replied, "No, by my honor, but I was told to come for you."

Rosalind asked, "Where did you learn that promise, fool?"

Touchstone explained, "From a certain knight. He swore by his honor they were good pancakes. And he swore by his honor the mustard was bad. Now I will insist, the pancakes were bad and the mustard was good. And yet the knight did not break his promise."

Celia asked, "How do you prove that, with all your great knowledge?"

Rosalind added, "Yes, indeed, now show us your wisdom."

Touchstone said, "Stand both of you forward now. Stroke your chins, and swear by your beards that I am a rascal."

Celia replied, "By our beards, if we had them, you are."

Touchstone said, "By my rascality, if I had it, then I would be. But if you swear by something that is not, you are not breaking your promise. No more was this knight swearing by his honor, for he never had any. Or if he had, he had sworn it away before he ever saw those pancakes or that mustard."

Celia asked, "Please, who do you mean?"

Touchstone answered, "One that old Frederick, your father, loves."

Celia said, "My father's love is enough to honor him. Enough! Speak no more of him. You will be whipped for teasing one of these days."

Touchstone remarked, "The more pity, that fools may not speak wisely about what wise men do foolishly."

Celia said, "By my truth, you say true. For since the little wit that fools have was silenced, the little foolishness that wise men have makes a great show. Here comes Monsieur Le Beau."

Rosalind observed, "With his mouth full of news."

Celia added, "Which he will put on us, as pigeons feed their young."

Rosalind said, "Then we shall be news-crammed."

Celia replied, "All the better; we shall be more interesting."

Le Beau entered.

Celia greeted him, "Good day, Monsieur Le Beau. What is the news?"

Le Beau said, "Fair princess, you have lost much good sport."

Celia asked, "Sport! Of what kind?"

Le Beau replied, "What kind, madam! How shall I answer you?"

Rosalind said, "As wit and fortune will."

Touchstone added, "Or as the Fates decide."

Celia commented, "Well said. That was laid on thickly."

Touchstone said, "Well, if I do not keep my place--"

Rosalind finished, "You lose your old smell."

Le Beau said, "You amaze me, ladies. I would have told you of good wrestling, which you have missed seeing."

Rosalind asked, "You tell us how the wrestling went."

Le Beau said, "I will tell you the beginning. And, if it pleases your ladyships, you may see the end. For the best is yet to happen. And here, where you are, they are coming to do it."

Celia said, "Well, the beginning, that is over and done with."

Le Beau began, "There comes an old man and his three sons--"

Celia interrupted, "I could match this beginning with an old tale."

Le Beau continued, "Three fine young men, of excellent growth and appearance."

Rosalind joked, "With signs on their necks, 'Be it known to all men by these papers.'"

Le Beau explained, "The eldest of the three wrestled with Charles, the duke's wrestler. Charles threw him in a moment and broke three of his ribs. There is little hope of life in him. He did the same to the second, and so the third. There they lie. The poor old man, their father, is making such sad cries over them. All the onlookers take his part with weeping."

Rosalind exclaimed, "Alas!"

Touchstone asked, "But what is the sport, monsieur, that the ladies have lost?"

Le Beau replied, "Why, this that I speak of."

Touchstone said, "Thus men may grow wiser every day. It is the first time I ever heard breaking of ribs was sport for ladies."

Celia agreed, "Or I, I promise you."

Rosalind asked, "But is there anyone else who wants to see this broken music in his sides? Is there yet another who loves rib-breaking? Shall we see this wrestling, cousin?"

Le Beau said, "You must, if you stay here. For here is the place chosen for the wrestling. And they are ready to perform it."

Celia said, "There, surely, they are coming. Let us now stay and see it."

Music played. Duke Frederick entered with Lords, Orlando, Charles, and Attendants.

Duke Frederick said, "Come on. Since the youth will not be persuaded, his own danger be on his eagerness."

Rosalind asked, "Is that the man over there?"

Le Beau confirmed, "Yes, madam."

Celia remarked, "Alas, he is too young! Yet he looks like he will succeed."

Duke Frederick asked, "How now, daughter and cousin! Have you crept here to see the wrestling?"

Rosalind replied, "Yes, my lord, if you please give us permission."

Duke Frederick said, "You will take little delight in it, I can tell you. There is such a difference in the men. In pity for the challenger's youth I would gladly talk him out of it. But he will not be persuaded. Speak to him, ladies. See if you can move him."

Celia said, "Call him here, good Monsieur Le Beau."

Duke Frederick ordered, "Do so. I will not be nearby."

Le Beau called, "Monsieur the challenger, the princesses call for you."

Orlando approached and said, "I attend them with all respect and duty."

Rosalind asked, "Young man, have you challenged Charles the wrestler?"

Orlando replied, "No, fair princess. He is the general challenger. I come only, as others do, to try the strength of my youth with him."

Celia said, "Young gentleman, your spirits are too bold for your years. You have seen cruel proof of this man's strength. If you saw yourself with your eyes or knew yourself with your judgment, the fear of your adventure would advise you to a more equal contest. We pray you, for your own sake, to choose your own safety and give up this attempt."

Rosalind added, "Do, young sir. Your reputation shall not be misjudged for it. We will ask the duke that the wrestling might not go forward."

Orlando said, "I beg you, do not punish me with your hard thoughts. I confess I am much guilty to deny such fair and excellent ladies anything. But let your fair eyes and gentle wishes go with me to my trial. If I am beaten, there is but one shamed who was never favored. If I pass away, it is but one person who was willing to be so. I shall do my friends no wrong, for I have none to mourn me. The world no injury, for in it I have nothing. I only fill up a place in the world. It may be better supplied when I have made it empty."

Rosalind said, "The little strength that I have, I wish it were with you."

Celia added, "And mine, to add to hers."

Rosalind said, "Fare you well. Pray heaven I am wrong about you!"

Celia wished, "May your heart's desires be with you!"

Charles called out, "Come, where is this young gallant that is so eager to lie with his mother earth?"

Orlando replied, "Ready, sir. But his wish has a more modest aim in it."

Duke Frederick announced, "You shall try but one fall."

Charles said, "No, I promise your grace, you shall not persuade him to a second. You have so strongly talked him out of a first."

Orlando retorted, "If you mean to mock me after, you should not have mocked me before. But come your ways."

Rosalind cried, "Now Hercules be your speed, young man!"

Celia wished, "I wish I were invisible, to catch the strong fellow by the leg."

They wrestled. The shouts of the crowd were as loud as a roaring lion.

Rosalind exclaimed, "Oh, excellent young man!"

Celia said, "If I had a thunderbolt in my eye, I can tell who would go down."

There was a shout. Charles was thrown.

Duke Frederick commanded, "No more, no more."

Orlando pleaded, "Yes, I beg your grace. I am not yet well warmed up."

Duke Frederick asked Charles, "How are you, Charles?"

Le Beau answered, "He cannot speak, my lord."

Duke Frederick ordered, "Bear him away. (To Orlando) What is your name, young man?"

Orlando replied, "Orlando, my lord. The youngest son of Sir Rowland de Boys."

Duke Frederick said, "I wish you had been son to some other man. The world thought your father honorable. But I always found him my enemy. You would have pleased me better with this deed if you had come from another house. But fare you well. You are a gallant youth. I wish you had told me of another father."

Duke Frederick, his train, and Le Beau left.

Celia asked, "Were I my father, cousin, would I do this?"

Orlando declared, "I am more proud to be Sir Rowland's son, his youngest son. I would not change that name to be adopted heir to Frederick." Rosalind felt her heart flutter like a trapped bird when she saw Orlando.

Rosalind said, "My father loved Sir Rowland as his own soul. And all the world agreed with my father. Had I known before this young man was his son, I should have given him tears with my pleas, before he should have risked this."

Celia said, "Gentle cousin, let us go thank him and encourage him. My father's rough and envious nature hurts my heart. Sir, you have done very well. If you keep your promises in love as justly as you have exceeded all promise here, your sweetheart shall be happy."

Rosalind, giving him a chain from her neck, said, "Gentleman, wear this for me. I am one out of favor with fortune. I could give more, but my hand lacks the means. Shall we go, coz?"

Celia replied, "Yes. Fare you well, fair gentleman."

Orlando thought, "Can I not say, I thank you? My better parts are all thrown down. And what stands here is but a practice dummy, a mere lifeless block."

Rosalind said, "(He calls us back.) My pride fell with my fortunes. I will ask him what he would. Did you call, sir? Sir, you have wrestled well and defeated more than your enemies."

Celia asked, "Will you go, coz?"

Rosalind replied, "I am with you. Fare you well."

Rosalind and Celia left.

Orlando wondered, "What feeling hangs these weights upon my tongue? I cannot speak to her, yet she invited conversation. Oh, poor Orlando, you are defeated! Either Charles or something weaker masters you."

Le Beau re-entered.

Le Beau said, "Good sir, I counsel you in friendship to leave this place. Although you have deserved high praise, true applause, and love, yet such is now the duke's mood that he misinterprets all that you have done. The duke is moody. What he is indeed, it is better for you to imagine than for me to speak of."

Orlando said, "I thank you, sir. And, please, tell me this: Which of the two was daughter of the duke that was here at the wrestling?"

Le Beau replied, "Neither his daughter, if we judge by manners. But yet indeed the shorter one is his daughter. The other is daughter to the banished duke. She is kept here by her uncle who took the dukedom, to keep his daughter company. Their loves are dearer than the natural bond of sisters. But I can tell you that lately this duke has taken displeasure against his gentle niece. It is based on no other reason but that the people praise her for her virtues and pity her for her good father's sake. And, on my life, his bad feelings against the lady will suddenly break forth. Sir, fare you well. Hereafter, in a better world than this, I shall desire more love and knowledge of you."

Orlando said, "I am much indebted to you. Fare you well."

Le Beau left.

Orlando thought, "Thus I must go from one bad situation to another. From a tyrant duke to a tyrant brother. But heavenly Rosalind!"

Orlando left.

SCENE 3

Celia and Rosalind were in a room in the palace. Rosalind's tears tasted salty on her lips.

Celia exclaimed, "Why, cousin! Why, Rosalind! Cupid have mercy! Not a word?"

Rosalind replied, "Not one to throw at a dog."

Celia said, "No, your words are too precious to be thrown away on dogs. Throw some of them at me. Come, make me lame with reasons."

Rosalind said, "Then there would be two cousins laid up. One would be lame with reasons, and the other mad without any."

Celia asked, "But is all this for your father?"

Rosalind replied, "No, some of it is for my child's father. Oh, how full of thorns is this working-day world!"

Celia said, "They are just burs, cousin, thrown on you in holiday fun. If we do not walk in the trodden paths, our very skirts will catch them."

Rosalind said, "I could shake them off my coat. These burs are in my heart."

Celia suggested, "Hum them away."

Rosalind wished, "I would try, if I could cry 'hem' and have him."

Celia urged, "Come, come, wrestle with your feelings."

Rosalind sighed, "Oh, they take the side of a better wrestler than myself!"

Celia said, "Oh, a good wish upon you! You will try in time, despite a fall. But, putting these jokes aside, let us talk seriously. Is it possible, so suddenly, you should fall into so strong a liking for old Sir Rowland's youngest son?"

Rosalind replied, "The duke my father loved his father dearly."

Celia asked, "Does it therefore follow that you should love his son dearly? By this kind of logic, I should hate him, for my father hated his father dearly. Yet I do not hate Orlando."

Rosalind said, "No, truly, do not hate him, for my sake."

Celia asked, "Why should I not? Does he not deserve well?"

Rosalind said, "Let me love him for that, and you love him because I do. Look, here comes the duke."

Celia observed, "With his eyes full of anger."

Duke Frederick entered with Lords.

Duke Frederick commanded Rosalind, "Mistress, leave with your safest speed. And get away from our court."

Rosalind asked, "Me, uncle?"

Duke Frederick replied, "You, cousin. Within these ten days if you are found as near our public court as twenty miles, you will die for it."

Rosalind pleaded, "I beg your grace, let me know my fault. If I understand myself or know my own desires, if I do not dream or am not frantic—as I trust I am not—then, dear uncle, never so much as in an unspoken thought did I offend your highness."

Duke Frederick stated, "Thus do all traitors. If their clearing of guilt consisted in words, they are as innocent as grace itself. Let it be enough for you that I do not trust you."

Rosalind argued, "Yet your mistrust cannot make me a traitor. Tell me what the likelihood depends on."

Duke Frederick said, "You are your father's daughter; there's enough."

Rosalind replied, "So was I when your highness took his dukedom. So was I when your highness banished him. Treason is not inherited, my lord. Or, if we did get it from our family, what is that to me? My father was no traitor. Then, good my lord, do not mistake me so much to think my poverty is treacherous."

Celia said, "Dear sovereign, hear me speak."

Duke Frederick replied, "Yes, Celia. We kept her for your sake. Else she would have gone along with her father."

Celia said, "I did not then beg to have her stay. It was your pleasure and your own pity. I was too young that time to value her. But now I know her. If she is a traitor, why so am I. We have always slept together, rose at the same time, learned, played, eaten together. And wherever we went, like Juno's swans, we always went coupled and inseparable."

Duke Frederick said, "She is too clever for you. And her smoothness, her very silence and her patience speak to the people, and they pity her. You are a fool. She robs you of your name. You will seem better and more virtuous when she is gone. Then do not open your lips. Firm and unchangeable is my judgment which I have passed upon her; she is banished." Celia was as loyal as a faithful puppy to Rosalind.

Celia declared, "Pronounce that sentence then on me, my lord. I cannot live out of her company."

Duke Frederick said, "You are a fool. (To Rosalind) You, niece, prepare yourself. If you stay past the time, upon my honor, and by the greatness of my word, you die."

Duke Frederick and Lords left.

Celia asked, "Oh my poor Rosalind, where will you go? Will you change fathers? I will give you mine. I tell you, do not be more grieved than I am."

Rosalind said, "I have more cause."

Celia replied, "You have not, cousin. Please be cheerful. Do you not know, the duke has banished me, his daughter?"

Rosalind said, "That he has not."

Celia said, "No, has not? Rosalind then lacks the love which teaches you that you and I are one. Shall we be separated? Shall we part, sweet girl? No. Let my father seek another heir. Therefore, plan with me how we may fly. Where to go and what to take with us. And do not try to take your troubles upon yourself, to bear your griefs yourself and leave me out. For, by this heaven, now pale at our sorrows, say what you can, I will go along with you."

Rosalind asked, "Why, where shall we go?"

Celia answered, "To seek my uncle in the forest of Arden."

Rosalind said, "Alas, what danger will it be to us, girls as we are, to travel so far! Beauty attracts thieves sooner than gold."

Celia planned, "I will put myself in poor and simple clothes. And with a kind of brown color, I will smudge my face. You do the same. So we shall pass along and never attract attackers."

Rosalind suggested, "Were it not better, because I am taller than common, that I dress myself all in men's clothes? A gallant axe upon my thigh, a boar-spear in my hand. And— in my heart, let whatever hidden woman's fear there be—we will have a bold and soldierly outside. As many other manly cowards have that face it out with their appearances."

Celia asked, "What shall I call you when you are a man?"

Rosalind replied, "I will have no worse name than Jove's own page. And therefore, make sure you call me Ganymede. But what will you be called?"

Celia decided, "Something that refers to my state. No longer Celia, but Aliena."

Rosalind asked, "But, cousin, what if we tried to steal the clownish fool out of your father's court? Would he not be a comfort to our travel?"

Celia said, "He will go along over the wide world with me. Leave me alone to persuade him. Let us go away, and get our jewels and our wealth together. Let us plan the best time and safest way to hide us from the chase that will be made after my flight. Now we go in happiness to liberty and not to banishment."

They left.

ACT II

SCENE 1

Duke Senior, Amiens, and two or three Lords dressed as foresters entered the Forest of Arden.

Duke Senior said, "Now, my friends and brothers in this new home. Has not our usual way of life here become sweeter than a fancy, showy life? Are not these woods safer than the jealous court?" He continued, "Here we only feel the changing seasons. Like the icy bite and the grumpy scolding of the winter's wind. When it bites and blows on my body, even till I shiver with cold, I smile. I say, 'This is not flattery. These are advisors that truly show me what I am.'" Duke Senior added, "Hard times can have good uses. Like an ugly toad that is not nice, but has a special jewel in its head. (It means even hard things can have something good inside, like finding a sweet berry on a thorny bush.) And this life, away from busy places, finds lessons in trees. It finds books in the running brooks. It finds talks in stones, and good in everything. I would not change it."

Amiens replied, "Your Grace is happy. You can turn bad luck into such a quiet and sweet way of living."

Duke Senior said, "Come, shall we go and get some deer meat for food?" He paused. "And yet it bothers me that the poor spotted deer, who live naturally in this wild place, should be hurt in their own home with sharp arrows."

The First Lord said, "Indeed, my lord. Sad Jaques is very upset about that. He even says you are more of a taker than your brother who sent you away." The First Lord continued, "Today, Lord Amiens and I quietly went behind him. He was lying under an oak tree. Its old root stuck out over the brook that rushes through this wood. A poor, lonely stag came to that place. It had been hurt by a hunter's arrow. It came there to rest sadly. Indeed, my lord, the poor animal made such loud groans. The sound almost seemed to stretch its skin to bursting. Big round tears chased each other down its innocent nose. It was a piteous sight. And so the hairy creature, much watched by sad Jaques, stood at the very edge of the fast brook. It was adding its tears to the water." The poor stag's groans were so loud, they almost burst its coat.

Duke Senior asked, "But what did Jaques say? Did he not find a lesson in this sight?"

The First Lord answered, "Oh, yes, he found a thousand lessons. First, about the deer crying into the stream that didn't need more water. 'Poor deer,' he said, 'you are like people in the world. You give what you have to those who already have too much.' Then, being there alone, left by his deer friends, Jaques said, 'That's right. This is how sadness separates friends.' Soon, a careless group of deer, full from eating grass, jumped past him. They never stopped to greet him. 'Yes,' said Jaques, 'Go on, you fat and comfortable citizens. That's just how it is. Why do you look at that poor, broken animal there?'" The First Lord added, "In this way, he strongly criticizes the country, the city, the court. Yes, and even our life here. He swears that we are just takers and mean people. He says it's worse to frighten the animals and hunt them in their own homes." Duke Senior thought the forest was much better than a stuffy palace, even with chilly winds!

Duke Senior asked, "And did you leave him thinking these things?"

A Second Lord said, "We did, my lord. He was weeping and talking about the sobbing deer."

Duke Senior said, "Show me the place. I love to talk with him in these sad moods. For then he is full of interesting thoughts."

The First Lord said, "I'll bring you to him right away."

They all left.

SCENE 2

Duke Frederick entered a room in the palace with his Lords.

Duke Frederick asked, "Can it be possible that no man saw them leave? It cannot be. Some bad people in my court must have agreed to this and allowed it."

The First Lord said, "I cannot hear of anyone who saw her. The ladies who attend her in her room saw her in bed. In the early morning, they found the bed empty of their mistress." Duke Frederick's voice boomed angrily in the grand room.

A Second Lord said, "My lord, the funny clown, whom your Grace often used to laugh at, is also missing. Hisperia, the princess's helper, admits that she secretly overheard your daughter and her cousin praising the wrestler very much.

The wrestler who recently beat strong Charles. And she believes, wherever they have gone, that young man is surely with them." Duke Frederick was not a happy camper when he found out the girls had vanished!

Duke Frederick ordered, "Send for his brother. Bring that young man here. If he is gone, bring his brother to me. I'll make him find him. Do this quickly. And let the search and questions not stop until these foolish runaways are brought back."

They all left.

SCENE 3

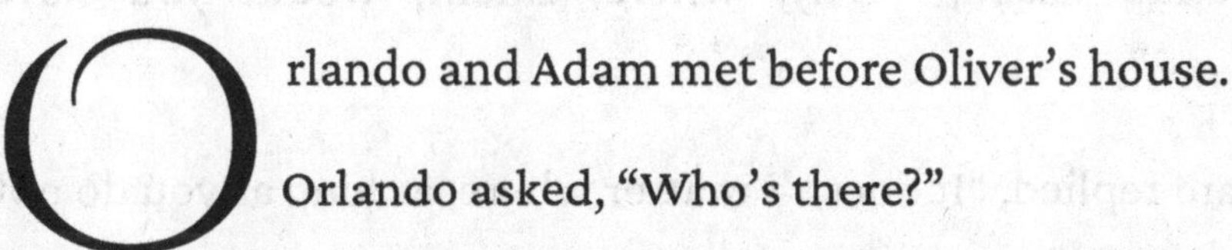

Orlando and Adam met before Oliver's house.

Orlando asked, "Who's there?"

Adam replied, "What, my young master? Oh, my gentle master! Oh my sweet master! Oh, you remind me of old Sir Rowland! Why, what are you doing here? Why are you so good? Why do people love you? And why are you gentle, strong, and brave? Why would you be so eager to beat the humorous Duke's strong fighter? News of your success has come home too quickly before you. Don't you know, master, that for some men their good qualities act as enemies? Yours do too. Your virtues, gentle master, are like holy traitors to you. Oh, what a world this is, when what is good harms the one who has it!" Adam's old voice trembled as he warned Orlando.

Orlando asked, "Why, what's the matter?"

Adam said, "Oh, unhappy youth! Do not come inside these doors. Within this house lives the enemy of all your good qualities. Your brother – no, not a brother. Yet the son – yet not the son, I will not call him son of him I was about to call his father – has heard of your praises. Tonight he means to burn the room where you usually sleep, with you in it. If he fails at that, he will have other ways to get rid of you. I over-heard him and his plans. This is no place. This house is like a butcher's shop. Hate it, fear it, do not enter it."

Orlando asked, "Why, where, Adam, would you have me go?"

Adam replied, "It doesn't matter where, as long as you do not come here."

Orlando asked, "What, would you have me go and beg for my food? Or with a rough sword take a thief's living on the common road? This I must do, or I do not know what to do. Yet this I will not do, no matter how I can. I would rather subject myself to the anger of a changed and angry brother."

Adam said, "But do not do so. I have five hundred crowns. It is the money I saved working for your father. I stored it to take care of me when my old body could no longer work. And when old age is ignored in corners. Take that. And may He who feeds the ravens, yes, who provides for the sparrow, be a comfort to my age! Here is the gold. And all this I give you. Let me be your servant. Though I look old, yet I am strong and healthy. For in my youth I never drank strong or harmful drinks. Nor did I foolishly seek out things that cause weakness. Therefore, my age is like a strong winter: frosty, but kind. Let me go with you. I'll do the service of a younger man in all your business and needs." Adam was like a super-grandpa, ready for an adventure!

Orlando said, "Oh, good old man, how well you show the constant service of the old world! Then, service was done for duty, not for reward! You are not like people today. Now, no one will work hard except for a promotion. And having that, they stop their service. It is not so with you. But, poor old man, you are trimming a rotten tree. It cannot even produce a blossom in return for all your pains and care. But come your ways. We will go along together. And before we have spent your youthful wages, we'll find some settled, simple happiness."

Adam said, "Master, go on, and I will follow you. To the last breath, with truth and loyalty. From seventeen years till now almost eighty, here I lived. But now I live here no more. At seventeen years, many seek their fortunes. But at eighty, it is too late. Yet fortune cannot reward me better than to pass away well and not owing my master anything."

They left.

SCENE 4

osalind (dressed as Ganymede), Celia (dressed as Aliena), and Touchstone entered the Forest of Arden.

Rosalind said, "Oh Jupiter, how tired my spirits are!"

Touchstone replied, "I do not care for my spirits, if my legs were not weary."

Rosalind said, "I could find it in my heart to shame my man's clothes and cry like a woman. But I must comfort the weaker person. My jacket and pants ought to show courage to her dress. Therefore, courage, good Aliena!"

Celia said, "I beg you, be patient with me. I cannot go any further."

Touchstone said, "For my part, I would rather be patient with you than carry you. Yet I should carry no heavy load if I did carry you. For I think you have no money in your purse."

Rosalind said, "Well, this is the forest of Arden." The forest floor was soft with fallen leaves under their tired feet.

Touchstone replied, "Yes, now I am in Arden. The more fool I. When I was at home, I was in a better place. But travelers must be content."

Rosalind said, "Yes, be so, good Touchstone."

Corin and Silvius entered, talking seriously.

Rosalind said, "Look you, who comes here. A young man and an old man in serious talk."

Corin said to Silvius, "That is the way to make her scorn you still."

Silvius cried, "Oh Corin, if you knew how I do love her!"

Corin replied, "I partly guess. For I have loved before now."

Silvius said, "No, Corin, being old, you cannot guess. Though in your youth you were as true a lover as ever sighed upon a midnight pillow. But if your love were ever like mine – as I am sure no man ever loved so much – how many very silly actions have you been drawn to by your imagination?"

Corin answered, "Into a thousand that I have forgotten."

Silvius exclaimed, "Oh, you did then never love so heartily! If you do not remember the slightest foolish thing that ever love made you run into, you have not loved. Or if you have not sat as I do now, tiring your listener with praise of your beloved, you have not loved. Or if you have not broken from company abruptly, as my strong feeling now makes me, you have not loved. Oh Phebe, Phebe, Phebe!" He then hurried away.

Rosalind said, "Alas, poor shepherd! Thinking of your hurt, I have by hard adventure found my own."

Touchstone said, "And I mine. I remember, when I was in love I broke my sword upon a stone. I told the stone to take that for coming at night to Jane Smile. And I remember kissing her washing stick. And the cow's udders that her pretty, chapped hands had milked. And I remember wooing a peapod instead of her. From it I took two peas and, giving them to her again, said with weeping tears, 'Wear these for my sake.' We that are true lovers run into strange actions. But as all is mortal in nature, so is all nature in love mortal in folly." Touchstone thought being in love made people do very silly things, like talking to peapods!

Rosalind said, "You speak wiser than you are aware of."

Touchstone replied, "No, I shall never be aware of my own cleverness until I break my shins against it."

Rosalind sighed, "Jove, Jove! This shepherd's strong feeling is much like mine."

Touchstone said, "And mine. But it grows a little old with me."

Celia said, "I beg you, one of you question that man. Ask if he for gold will give us any food. I faint almost to the point of passing away."

Touchstone called out, "Hello, you clown!"

Rosalind said, "Peace, fool. He is not your relative."

Corin asked, "Who calls?"

Touchstone replied, "Your betters, sir."

Corin said, "Else are they very wretched."

Rosalind said, "Peace, I say. Good evening to you, friend."

Corin replied, "And to you, gentle sir, and to you all."

Rosalind asked, "I beg you, shepherd, if love or gold can in this wild place buy food and lodging, bring us where we may rest ourselves and feed. Here's a young maid very tired from travel. She faints for help."

Corin said, "Fair sir, I pity her. And wish, for her sake more than for my own, my fortunes were more able to help her. But I am shepherd to another man. I do not shear the fleeces that I graze. My master is of a mean nature. He little cares to find the way to heaven by doing kind deeds for guests. Besides, his cottage, his flocks, and areas of pasture are now for sale. And at our sheep-house now, because of his absence, there is nothing that you will feed on. But what there is, come see. And in my voice, most welcome shall you be."

Rosalind asked, "Who is he that shall buy his flock and pasture?"

Corin answered, "That young man that you saw here just a while ago. He cares little for buying anything."

Rosalind said, "I beg you, if it is honest, buy the cottage, pasture, and the flock. And you shall have money from us to pay for it."

Celia added, "And we will improve your wages. I like this place. And willingly could waste my time in it."

Corin said, "Certainly the thing is to be sold. Go with me. If you like, upon report, the soil, the profit, and this kind of life, I will be your very faithful worker. And I will buy it with your gold right away."

They all left.

SCENE 5

Amiens, Jaques, and others entered the Forest.

Amiens sang a song. "Under the green tree, who likes to lie with me? And sing a happy tune like a sweet bird sings? Come here, come here, come here. Here you will see no enemy. Only winter and stormy weather." Amiens' song echoed sweetly among the tall green trees.

Jaques said, "More, more, I beg you, more."

Amiens replied, "It will make you sad, Monsieur Jaques."

Jaques said, "I thank it. More, I beg you, more. I can get sadness out of a song, as a weasel drinks eggs. More, I beg you, more." Jaques liked sad songs so much, he said he could get sadness out of them like a weasel drinks an egg! How strange!

Amiens said, "My voice is rough. I know I cannot please you."

Jaques replied, "I do not desire you to please me. I do desire you to sing. Come, more. Another verse. Do you call them verses?"

Amiens said, "Whatever you will, Monsieur Jaques."

Jaques said, "No, I care not for their names. They owe me nothing. Will you sing?"

Amiens replied, "More at your request than to please myself."

Jaques said, "Well then, if ever I thank any man, I'll thank you. But what they call politeness is like the meeting of two dog-faced monkeys. And when a man thanks me heartily, I think I have given him a penny and he gives me poor thanks. Come, sing. And you that will not, hold your tongues."

Amiens said, "Well, I'll end the song. Sirs, set the table while I sing. The Duke will eat under this tree. He has been all this day looking for you."

Jaques said, "And I have been all this day trying to avoid him. He is too argumentative for my company. I think of as many matters as he. But I give heaven thanks and make no boast of them. Come, sing, come."

Amiens sang again. "Who avoids ambition and loves to live in the sun? Seeking the food he eats and pleased with what he gets? Come here, come here, come here. Here he will see no enemy. Only winter and stormy weather."

Jaques said, "I'll give you a verse to this tune that I made yesterday, despite my lack of trying."

Amiens replied, "And I'll sing it."

Jaques said, "Thus it goes: If it ever happens that a man acts like a silly donkey. Leaving his money and comfort, just to be stubborn. Ducdame, ducdame, ducdame. Here he will see big fools like him, if he will come to me."

Amiens asked, "What's that 'ducdame'?"

Jaques explained, "'Tis a Greek magic word, to call fools into a circle. I'll go sleep, if I can. If I cannot, I'll complain against all the first-born children of Egypt."

Amiens said, "And I'll go seek the Duke. His meal is prepared."

They left by different ways.

SCENE 6

Orlando and Adam entered the forest.

Adam said, "Dear master, I can go no further. Oh, I am so hungry! Here I lie down. I feel I might pass away. Farewell, kind master." The chilly forest air made Adam shiver as he lay on the ground.

Orlando replied, "Why, how now, Adam! Do you not have more strength in you? Live a little. Comfort yourself a little. Cheer up a little. If this wild forest has anything wild, I will either be food for it or bring it for food to you. Your idea of passing away is nearer than your strength is. For my sake, be comfortable. Hold off feeling so bad for a while. I will be here with you soon. And if I do not bring you something to eat, I will give you leave to rest. But if you pass away before I come, you are making fun of my labor. Well said! You look more cheerful. And I'll be with you quickly. Yet you lie in the cold air. Come, I will carry you to some shelter. And you shall not pass away for lack of a dinner, if there is anything alive in this wilderness. Cheer up, good Adam!" Orlando was a true friend, promising to find food for Adam, even if it was hard!

They left.

SCENE 7

A table was set out in the forest. Duke Senior, Amiens, and Lords dressed like outlaws entered.

Duke Senior said, "I think he has turned into an animal. For I can nowhere find him like a man."

The First Lord said, "My lord, he just now went from here. Here he was merry, hearing a song."

Duke Senior replied, "If he, who is full of arguments, grows musical, we shall soon have discord in the heavens. Go, seek him. Tell him I would speak with him."

Jaques entered.

The First Lord said, "He saves my labor by his own approach."

Duke Senior asked, "Why, how now, monsieur! What a life is this, that your poor friends must beg for your company? What, you look merry!"

Jaques exclaimed, "A fool, a fool! I met a fool in the forest. A jester! A miserable world! As I live by food, I met a fool. He laid him down and warmed himself in the sun. And complained about Lady Fortune in good terms. In good clear terms, and yet a jester. 'Good morrow, fool,' I said. 'No, sir,' he replied. 'Call me not fool till heaven has sent me fortune.' And then he took a sundial from his pocket. And, looking on it with a dull eye, he said very wisely, 'It is ten o'clock. Thus we may see how the world wags. 'Tis but an hour ago since it was nine. And after one hour more 'twill be eleven. And so, from hour to hour, we grow and grow. And then, from hour to hour, we get old and older. And thereby hangs a tale.' When I heard the jester thus speak wisely on time, my lungs began to crow like a rooster. That fools should be so deep in thought! And I did laugh without stopping for an hour by his sundial. Oh, noble fool! A worthy fool! A jester's clothes are the only thing to wear."

Duke Senior asked, "What fool is this?"

Jaques replied, "Oh, worthy fool! One that has been a courtier. And says, if ladies are young and pretty, they have the gift to know it. And in his brain, which is as dry as a left-over biscuit after a sea trip, he has strange places crammed with observation. He shares these in jumbled ways. Oh, that I were a fool! I am ambitious for a jester's coat."

Duke Senior said, "You shall have one."

Jaques said, "It is my only wish. Provided that you clear your better judgments of all opinion that I am wise. I must have liberty also, as large a permission as the wind, to blow on whom I please. For so fools have. And they that are most annoyed with my folly, they most must laugh. And why, sir, must they so? The 'why' is plain as the way to the village church. He that a fool cleverly teases, acts very foolishly, although he is smarting, not to seem unaware of the joke. If not, the wise man's folly is revealed even by the quick glances of the fool. Dress me in my jester's coat. Give me leave to speak my mind. And I will through and through cleanse the foul body of the infected world, if they will patiently receive my medicine."

Duke Senior said, "Shame on you! I can tell what you would do."

Jaques asked, "What, for a coin, would I do but good?"

Duke Senior replied, "Most mischievous foul sin, in scolding sin. For you yourself have been a wild person. As pleasure-seeking as an animal. And all the bad habits that you with free foot have caught, you would spread into the general world."

Jaques asked, "Why, who cries out on pride, that can in that tax any private person? Does it not flow as hugely as the sea, till the means do ebb? What woman in the city do I name, when I say the city-woman bears the cost of princes on unworthy shoulders? Who can come in and say that I mean her, when such a one as she is her neighbor? Or what is he of lowest job that says his finery is not of my cost, thinking that I mean him, but therein suits his folly to my words? There then; how then? what then? Let me see wherein my tongue has wronged him. If it does him right, then he has wronged himself. If he is free from blame, why then my words fly like a wild goose, unclaimed by any man. But who comes here?"

Orlando entered, with his sword drawn. The smell of roasting meat drifted from the Duke's outdoor table.

Orlando commanded, "Stop, and eat no more."

Jaques replied, "Why, I have eaten none yet."

Orlando said, "Nor shall you, till necessity be served."

Jaques asked, "Of what kind should this rooster come from?"

Duke Senior asked, "Are you made bold like this, man, by your distress? Or else are you a rude despiser of good manners, that in politeness you seem so empty?"

Orlando replied, "You understood my feeling at first. The thorny point of bare distress has taken from me the show of smooth politeness. Yet I am well-bred and know some good manners. But stop, I say. He dies that touches any of this fruit till I and my needs are answered."

Jaques said, "If you will not be answered with reason, I must be in trouble."

Duke Senior asked, "What would you have? Your gentleness shall force us more than your force will move us to gentleness."

Orlando said, "I almost pass away for food. And let me have it."

Duke Senior replied, "Sit down and feed. And welcome to our table."

Orlando said, "Do you speak so gently? Pardon me, I pray you. I thought that all things had been savage here. And therefore I put on the look of stern command. But whatever you are that in this desert, hard to reach, under the shade of melancholy boughs, lose and neglect the creeping hours of time— If ever you have looked on better days, if ever been where bells have rung for church, if ever sat at any good man's feast, if ever from your eyelids wiped a tear and know what it is to pity and be pitied, let gentleness be my strong request. In this hope I blush, and hide my sword."

Duke Senior said, "True is it that we have seen better days. And have with holy bell been called to church. And sat at good men's feasts and wiped our eyes of drops that sacred pity has created. And therefore sit you down in gentleness. And take by command what help we have that to your wanting may be given."

Orlando said, "Then but wait to eat your food a little while. While, like a mother deer, I go to find my young one and give it food. There is an old poor man, who after me has many a weary step limped in pure love. Till he be first satisfied, troubled with two weak evils, age and hunger, I will not touch a bit."

Duke Senior said, "Go find him out. And we will waste nothing till you return."

Orlando replied, "I thank you. And be blessed for your good comfort!" He left.

Duke Senior said, "You see we are not all alone unhappy. This wide and universal theater presents more sad shows than the scene wherein we play in."

Jaques said, "All the world's a stage. And all the men and women merely players. They have their exits and their entrances. And one man in his time plays many parts. His acts being seven ages. At first the infant, crying and being a bit sick in the nurse's arms. And then the whining school-boy, with his satchel and bright morning face, creeping like a snail unwillingly to school. And then the lover, sighing very deeply, with a sad poem made to his sweetheart's eyebrow. Then a soldier, full of strange promises and with a wild, spotted beard, jealous in honor, sudden and quick in quarrel, seeking quick fame even if it was dangerous like facing a cannon. And then the justice, in a fair round belly with good chicken lined, with serious eyes and beard of formal cut, full of wise sayings and modern examples. And so he plays his part. The sixth age shifts into the thin old man in slippers, with spectacles on his nose and pouch on his side. His youthful pants, well saved, are a world too wide for his shrunk leg. And his big manly voice, turning again toward a childish high voice, pipes and whistles in his sound. Last scene of all, that ends this strange eventful history, is second childishness and mere forgetfulness. Without teeth, without seeing well, without tasting well, without much of anything." Jaques thought life was like a big play with seven acts, from a tiny baby to a very old person!

Orlando re-entered, with Adam.

Duke Senior said, "Welcome. Set down your respected burden. And let him feed."

Orlando replied, "I thank you most for him."

Adam said, "So you should. I scarce can speak to thank you for myself."

Duke Senior said, "Welcome. Begin to eat. I will not trouble you as yet, to question you about your fortunes. Give us some music. And, good cousin, sing."

Amiens sang. "Blow, blow, you winter wind. You are not as mean as when people are not thankful. Your bite is not so sharp. This is because you are not seen. Even if your breath is rough. Heigh-ho! Sing heigh-ho! To the green holly. Most friendship is pretending. Most loving is just silly. Then, heigh-ho, the holly! This life is very happy. Freeze, freeze, you bitter sky. You do not hurt as much as forgotten kindness. Though you make the water freeze, your sting is not as sharp as a friend who is forgotten. Heigh-ho! Sing, and so on."

Duke Senior said to Orlando, "If you are the good Sir Rowland's son, as you have whispered faithfully you were, and as my eye sees his likeness most truly drawn and living in your face, be truly welcome here. I am the Duke that loved your father. The rest of your fortune, go to my cave and tell me. Good old man," he said to Adam, "you are as welcome as your master is. Support him by the arm." He took Orlando's hand. "Give me your hand, and let me understand all your fortunes."

They all left.

ACT III

SCENE 1

Duke Frederick, some Lords, and Oliver came into a room in the palace.

Duke Frederick said, "You have not seen him since? Sir, that cannot be true." He looked sternly at Oliver. "If I were not a kind man, I would punish you now. You are here, but your brother Orlando is not. But listen to me. Find your brother, wherever he is. Search for him everywhere. Bring him to me, alive or not, within one year. Or you cannot live here anymore. Your lands and all your things will be taken by us. We will keep them until your brother says you are not to blame for what we think you did." The Duke's voice was loud, like a drum beating. Oliver looked as scared as a mouse caught by a cat.

Oliver said, "Oh, I wish your Highness knew my heart in this! I never loved my brother in my life."

Duke Frederick replied, "Then you are even more of a bad person. Well, push him out of the doors. Let my officers take his house and lands. Do this quickly and send him away."

Then they all left.

SCENE 2

In the forest, Orlando walked alone with a paper in his hand.

Orlando said, "Hang there, my poem, to show my love." He looked up at the sky. "And you, moon, look down with your gentle eye. See your follower's name, Rosalind. She rules my whole life. Oh Rosalind! These trees will be my books. I will write my thoughts on their bark. Every eye that looks in this forest will see your goodness everywhere. Run, run, Orlando! Carve on every tree about her. She is fair, pure, and more wonderful than words can say." The poems he hung rustled like dry leaves in the wind.

Orlando left.

Then Corin and Touchstone came into the forest.

Corin asked, "And how do you like this shepherd's life, Master Touchstone?"

Touchstone replied, "Truly, shepherd, it is a good life by itself. But because it is a shepherd's life, it is not good. Because it is lonely, I like it very well. But because it is private, it is a very bad life. Now, because it is in the fields, it pleases me well. But because it is not in the court, it is boring. As it is a simple life, you see, I like it. But as there is not much in it, I do not like it much. Do you know any wise things, shepherd?" Touchstone thought being a shepherd was as dull as a rainy day with no games.

Corin said, "Only that I know the sicker someone is, the worse he feels. And someone without money, tools, and happiness is without three good friends. Rain makes things wet. Fire burns. Good grass makes fat sheep. A big reason for night is that the sun is gone. Someone not smart by nature or learning might complain about his family. Or he comes from a dull family."

Touchstone said, "Such a person is a natural thinker. Were you ever at court, shepherd?"

Corin answered, "No, truly."

Touchstone said, "Then you are in trouble."

Corin replied, "No, I hope not."

Touchstone said, "Truly, you are in trouble. Like a badly cooked egg, all on one side."

Corin asked, "For not being at court? What is your reason?"

Touchstone explained, "Why, if you were never at court, you never saw good manners. If you never saw good manners, then your manners must be bad. Badness is wrong, and wrongness leads to trouble. You are in a tricky situation, shepherd."

Corin said, "Not at all, Touchstone. Good manners at court seem silly in the country. Country behavior is made fun of at court. You told me you do not greet by bowing at court. But you kiss your hands. That would be unclean if courtiers were shepherds."

Touchstone said, "Give an example, quickly. Come, an example."

Corin replied, "Why, we are always handling our sheep. And their wool, you know, is oily."

Touchstone said, "Why, do not your courtier's hands sweat? And is not sheep oil as wholesome as a man's sweat? Silly, silly. A better example, I say. Come."

Corin said, "Besides, our hands are hard."

Touchstone replied, "Your lips will feel them sooner. Silly again. A better example, come."

Corin said, "And they are often covered with tar from caring for our sheep. Would you have us kiss tar? The courtier's hands are perfumed."

Touchstone exclaimed, "Most silly man! You are like a worm next to good meat! Learn from the wise: perfume from a civet cat is not as good as tar. Tar is simpler. Give a better example, shepherd."

Corin said, "You have too much court wit for me. I will rest."

Touchstone asked, "Will you rest in trouble? You need help, simple man! You are not wise."

Corin said, "Sir, I am a true worker. I earn what I eat. I get what I wear. I owe no man hate. I do not envy any man's happiness. I am glad for other men's good. I am content with my troubles. My greatest pride is to see my ewes graze and my lambs drink milk."

Touchstone said, "That is another simple wrong in you. To bring ewes and rams together. To get your living by animals having babies. To help a male sheep find a young female sheep. That is not a good match. If you are not in trouble for this, then no shepherd will be. I cannot see how you will escape."

Corin said, "Here comes young Master Ganymede, my new mistress's brother."

Rosalind entered, reading a paper.

Rosalind read, "From far away east to far away west, no jewel is like Rosalind. Her goodness travels on the wind. All the world knows Rosalind is good. All the prettiest pictures look dull next to Rosalind. Let no one beautiful be kept in mind but the beautiful Rosalind."

Touchstone said, "I can rhyme like that for eight years. Except during dinner, supper, and sleeping. It sounds like simple women going to market."

Rosalind said, "Go away, fool!"

Touchstone said, "For a taste: If a deer needs a friend, let him find Rosalind. If a cat likes its own kind, so will Rosalind. Winter clothes must be lined, so must thin Rosalind. Those who harvest must gather and tie, then put Rosalind in the cart. The sweetest nut has the sourest shell, such a nut is Rosalind. He who finds the sweetest rose must find love's thorn and Rosalind. These poems are not very good. Why do you bother with them?"

Rosalind said, "Quiet, you dull fool! I found them on a tree."

Touchstone replied, "Truly, the tree gives bad fruit."

Rosalind said, "I will mix your words with the tree. Then I shall mix it with a medlar fruit. Then it will be the earliest fruit in the country. For you will be soft before you are half ripe. That is the way of the medlar."

Touchstone said, "You have spoken. But whether wisely or not, let the forest decide."

Celia entered with a paper.

Rosalind said, "Quiet! Here comes my sister, reading. Stand aside."

Celia read, "'Why should this be a desert? Because no people are here? No. I will hang messages on every tree. They will show kind words. Some, how short man's life is. It is like a short journey. His whole life is like a hand's width. Some, about broken promises between friends. But on the prettiest branches, or at every sentence end, I will write Rosalinda. Teaching all who read to know the best of every spirit. Heaven wanted to show this in one person. So Heaven told Nature to fill one body with all good things. Nature then gathered Helen's pretty cheek, but not her tricky heart. Cleopatra's royal way. Atalanta's good skills. Sad Lucretia's shyness. Thus Rosalind of many parts was planned by heaven. With many faces, eyes, and hearts, to have the most prized qualities. Heaven wanted her to have these gifts. And I to live and die her servant.'"

Rosalind said, "Oh, what a long, boring love speech you have given! And you never said, 'Have patience, good people!'"

Celia said, "What now! Back, friends! Shepherd, go off a little. Go with him, sirrah."

Touchstone said, "Come, shepherd, let us make a proper retreat. Not with everything, but with our bags."

Corin and Touchstone left.

Celia asked, "Did you hear these poems?"

Rosalind answered, "Oh, yes, I heard them all, and more too. For some of them had too many beats for the lines."

Celia said, "That does not matter. The beats could carry the poems."

Rosalind replied, "Yes, but the beats were weak. They could not stand without the poem. So they stood weakly in the poem."

Celia asked, "But did you hear without wondering how your name was hung and carved on these trees?"

Rosalind said, "I was already wondering about it for a long time before you came. For look here what I found on a palm tree. I have never had so many rhymes written about me. Not since a very old story about an Irish rat, which I can hardly remember."

Celia asked, "Do you know who did this?"

Rosalind asked, "Is it a man?"

Celia said, "And he wears a chain that you once wore, around his neck. Are you blushing?"

Rosalind asked, "Please, who?"

Celia said, "Oh dear, oh dear! It is hard for friends to meet. But mountains can be moved by earthquakes and so meet."

Rosalind insisted, "No, but who is it?"

Celia asked, "Is it possible?"

Rosalind begged, "No, I ask you now with great urgency, tell me who it is."

Celia exclaimed, "Oh wonderful, wonderful, and most wonderful wonderful! And again wonderful, and after that, beyond all shouting!"

Rosalind said, "Oh my goodness! Do you think because I wear boy's clothes, I do not have feelings like a girl? Waiting any longer feels like a very long journey. Please, tell me who it is quickly. Speak fast. I wish you would just say his name quickly! Please, take the cork out of your mouth so I may hear your news."

Celia said, "So you can hear all about this man."

Rosalind asked, "Is he made by God? What kind of man? Is he handsome? Does he have a beard?"

Celia answered, "No, he has only a little beard."

Rosalind said, "Why, God will send more, if the man will be thankful. Let me wait for his beard to grow. But tell me about his chin now."

Celia said, "It is young Orlando. He beat the wrestler. And he won your heart very quickly."

Rosalind said, "No, stop teasing. Tell me seriously and truthfully."

Celia replied, "Truly, cousin, it is he."

Rosalind whispered, "Orlando?"

Celia confirmed, "Orlando."

Rosalind cried, "Oh dear! What shall I do in these boy's clothes? What did he do when you saw him? What did he say? How did he look? What was he wearing? What is he doing here? Did he ask for me? Where is he staying? How did he leave you? And when will you see him again? Answer me quickly!"

Celia said, "You must borrow a giant's mouth first! That is too much to answer in one word. To say yes and no to these questions is more than answering a list of questions."

Rosalind asked, "But does he know that I am in this forest and in man's clothes? Does he look as fresh as he did the day he wrestled?"

Celia replied, "It is easier to count tiny specks of dust than to understand a lover's questions. But have a taste of my finding him. And enjoy it with good attention. I found him under a tree, like a dropped acorn."

Rosalind said, "It may well be called Jove's tree, when it drops such fruit."

Celia said, "Listen to me, good madam."

Rosalind replied, "Go on."

Celia continued, "There he lay, stretched out, like a wounded knight."

Rosalind said, "Though it is sad to see such a sight, it suits the ground well."

Celia said, "Please, stop your tongue. It is talking too much at the wrong time. He was dressed like a hunter."

Rosalind exclaimed, "Oh, this is a bad sign! He comes to make me fall more in love."

Celia said, "I want to tell my story simply. You keep interrupting and confusing me."

Rosalind said, "Do you not know I am a woman? When I think, I must speak. Sweet, say on."

Celia said, "You confuse me. Soft! Is he not coming here?"

Orlando and Jaques entered.

Rosalind whispered to Celia, "It is he. Let's hide and watch him."

Jaques said to Orlando, "I thank you for your company. But, truly, I would rather have been alone."

Orlando replied, "And so would I. But yet, for politeness, I thank you too for your company."

Jaques said, "Goodbye. Let's not meet often."

Orlando said, "I hope we become even more like strangers."

Jaques said, "I ask you, do not spoil more trees by carving love songs on them."

Orlando replied, "I ask you, do not spoil my poems by reading them badly."

Jaques asked, "Rosalind is your love's name?"

Orlando answered, "Yes, exactly."

Jaques said, "I do not like her name."

Orlando replied, "No one thought of pleasing you when she was named."

Jaques asked, "What height is she?"

Orlando answered, "Just as high as my heart."

Jaques said, "You are full of pretty answers. Have you known ladies and tricked them out of their rings with clever words?"

Orlando replied, "Not so. But my answers are simple, like the sayings on wall hangings. Your questions are like those too."

Jaques said, "You are quick-witted. I think your wit is as fast as Atalanta's feet. Will you sit down with me? And we two will complain about the world and our troubles."

Orlando said, "I will only find fault with myself. I know my own mistakes best."

Jaques said, "The worst fault you have is to be in love."

Orlando replied, "It is a fault I will not change for your best good quality. I am tired of you."

Jaques said, "Truly, I was looking for a fool when I found you."

Orlando replied, "The fool is in the stream. Look in and you will see him."

Jaques said, "There I shall see my own reflection."

Orlando said, "Which I think is either a fool or nothing."

Jaques said, "I will stay no longer with you. Farewell, good Sir Love."

Orlando replied, "I am glad you are leaving. Goodbye, good Mister Melancholy."

Jaques left.

Rosalind said to Celia, "(Aside) I will talk to him like a cheeky servant. In these clothes, I will tease him. Do you hear, forester?"

Orlando replied, "Very well. What do you want?"

Rosalind asked, "I ask you, what time is it by the clock?"

Orlando said, "You should ask me what time of day it is. There is no clock in the forest."

Rosalind replied, "Then there is no true lover in the forest. Or else sighing every minute and groaning every hour would show how slowly Time passes, just like a clock."

Orlando asked, "And why not the swift foot of Time? Would that not have been as right?"

Rosalind said, "By no means, sir. Time moves at different speeds for different people. I will tell you who Time walks slowly with. Who Time trots with. Who Time gallops with. And who he stands still with."

Orlando asked, "Please, who does he trot with?"

Rosalind answered, "Well, he trots hard with a young maid.

Between her engagement and her wedding day. If it is only a week, Time moves so slowly it feels like seven years."

Orlando asked, "Who does Time walk slowly with?"

Rosalind replied, "With a priest who does not know Latin. And a rich man who is not sick. One sleeps because he cannot study. The other lives happily because he feels no pain. One does not have the burden of hard learning. The other knows no burden of heavy, boring poverty. Time walks slowly with these."

Orlando asked, "Who does he gallop with?"

Rosalind answered, "With a thief going to be punished. For though he goes as softly as he can, he thinks he gets there too soon."

Orlando asked, "Who does Time stay still with?"

Rosalind replied, "With lawyers on holiday. For they sleep between work terms. Then they do not notice how Time moves."

Orlando asked, "Where do you live, pretty youth?"

Rosalind answered, "With this shepherdess, my sister. Here on the edge of the forest. Like fringe on a skirt."

Orlando asked, "Are you from this place?"

Rosalind replied, "Like a rabbit that lives where it was born."

Orlando said, "You speak more finely than someone from such a faraway place."

Rosalind said, "Many have told me so. But indeed, an old, good uncle of mine taught me to speak. He used to live in the town in his youth. He knew about love too well, for he fell in love there. I have heard him give many talks against it. And I thank God I am not a woman. To have so many silly faults that he said all women have."

Orlando asked, "Can you remember any of the main bad things he said about women?"

Rosalind replied, "There were no main ones. They were all similar, like coins. Every fault seemed huge until the next fault came to match it."

Orlando said, "Please, tell me some of them."

Rosalind said, "No, I will only give my advice to those who need it. There is a man who wanders the forest. He harms our young plants by carving 'Rosalind' on their barks. He hangs poems on hawthorns and sad songs on brambles. All, indeed, treating the name Rosalind like she is a goddess. If I could meet that love-sick man, I would give him some good advice. For he seems to have a daily fever of love."

Orlando said, "I am he that is so love-shaken. I ask you, tell me your cure."

Rosalind said, "You do not have any of my uncle's signs. He taught me how to know a man in love. I am sure you are not a prisoner in that cage of rushes."

Orlando asked, "What were his signs?"

Rosalind listed, "A thin cheek, which you do not have. A sad, sunken eye, which you do not have. A worried mind, which you do not have. A messy beard, which you do not have. But I forgive you for that. For simply, your small beard is like a younger brother's small income. Then your stockings should be falling down. Your hat plain. Your sleeve unbuttoned. Your shoe untied. Everything about you should look messy and sad. But you are no such man. You are very neat in your clothes. You look like you love yourself, not someone else."

Orlando said, "Fair youth, I wish I could make you believe I love."

Rosalind replied, "Me believe it! You may as soon make her that you love believe it. Which, I promise, she is more likely to do than to admit she does. That is one of the ways women often say what they do not truly feel. But, in truth, are you he that hangs the poems on the trees, where Rosalind is so admired?"

Orlando swore, "I swear to you, youth, by the white hand of Rosalind, I am that he. That unfortunate he."

Rosalind asked, "But are you as much in love as your rhymes say?"

Orlando answered, "Neither rhyme nor reason can express how much."

Rosalind said, "Love is just a kind of silliness. And, I tell you, it deserves to be treated like other kinds of silliness. And the reason why they are not so punished and cured is that this silliness is so common. Even the people who might help are in love too. Yet I claim to cure it by advice."

Orlando asked, "Did you ever cure anyone so?"

Rosalind replied, "Yes, one, and in this way. He was to imagine me as his love, his mistress. And I made him come every day to woo me. At which time I would act like a changeable youth. I would be sad, silly, always changing my mind. I would want things, then not want them. I would be proud, then act strangely. I would cry, then smile. For every feeling something, and for no feeling truly anything. As boys and women mostly are. I would like him now, then dislike him. Then be nice to him, then reject him. Now weep for him, then spit at him. I made my suitor change from being silly with love to being truly unhappy. He wanted to leave the world and live alone quietly. And thus I cured him. And this way I will try to clean all the love out of you. Like washing a sheep's heart very clean. So there will not be one spot of love in it."

Orlando said, "I would not be cured, youth."

Rosalind said, "I would cure you, if you would just call me Rosalind. And come every day to my cottage and woo me."

Orlando declared, "Now, by the faith of my love, I will. Tell me where it is."

Rosalind said, "Go with me to it and I will show it to you. And on the way you shall tell me where in the forest you live. Will you go?"

Orlando answered, "With all my heart, good youth."

Rosalind said, "No, you must call me Rosalind. Come, sister, will you go?"

They all left.

SCENE 3

In the forest, Touchstone and Audrey entered. Jaques was behind them, hiding.

Touchstone said, "Come quickly, good Audrey. I will fetch your goats, Audrey. And how, Audrey? Am I the man yet? Do you like my plain looks?"

Audrey exclaimed, "Your looks! Lord help us! What looks!"

Touchstone said, "I am here with you and your goats. Like the playful poet Ovid was among the Goths, who did not understand him."

Jaques said to himself, "(Aside) Oh, wisdom in the wrong place! It is worse than a great king in a tiny hut!"

Touchstone continued, "When people do not understand a man's poems or his jokes, it is very bad. It is worse than getting a big bill in a small inn. Truly, I wish the gods had made you like poetry."

Audrey said, "I do not know what 'poetical' is. Is it honest in actions and words? Is it a true thing?"

Touchstone replied, "No, truly. For the truest poetry is the most pretend. And lovers like poetry. What they swear in poetry, as lovers, they may be pretending." Audrey was as simple as a daisy in a field.

Audrey asked, "Do you wish then that the gods had made me like poetry?"

Touchstone said, "I do, truly. For you swear to me you are honest. Now, if you were a poet, I might have some hope you were only pretending."

Audrey asked, "Would you not have me honest?"

Touchstone replied, "No, truly, unless you were plain-looking. For honesty with beauty is like adding honey to sugar – too much sweetness."

Jaques said to himself, "(Aside) A fool who says wise things by accident!"

Audrey said, "Well, I am not pretty. And therefore I pray the gods make me honest."

Touchstone said, "Truly, and to give honesty to a plain girl is like putting good food on a dirty plate."

Audrey replied, "I am not messy, though I thank the gods I am plain."

Touchstone said, "Well, praised be the gods for your plainness! Messiness might come later. But however it may be, I will marry you. For that, I have been with Sir Oliver Martext. He is the vicar of the next village. He has promised to meet me in this place of the forest and to marry us." The leaves crunched under their feet as they walked.

Jaques said to himself, "(Aside) I would like to see this meeting."

Audrey said, "Well, may the gods give us joy!"

Touchstone said, "Amen. A man, if he were scared, might hesitate in this. For here we have no church, only the woods. No guests, only animals with horns. But what then? Courage! He said, 'Courage! Even if things seem difficult, we must be brave.' It is good to be married. Here comes Sir Oliver."

Sir Oliver Martext entered.

Touchstone said, "Sir Oliver Martext, you are well met. Will you marry us here under this tree? Or shall we go with you to your chapel?"

Sir Oliver Martext asked, "Is there no one here to give the bride away?"

Touchstone replied, "I will not take her as a gift from any man."

Sir Oliver Martext said, "Truly, she must be given, or the marriage is not lawful."

Jaques came forward and said, "Proceed, proceed. I will give her."

Touchstone said, "Good evening, good Master What-is-your-name. How do you do, sir? You are very well met. Thank you for your company last time. I am very glad to see you. Just a small matter here, sir. No, please keep your hat on."

Jaques asked, "Will you be married, fool?"

Touchstone replied, "As the ox has its yoke, sir, the horse its bridle, and the falcon her bells, so man has his wishes. And like pigeons kiss, marriage is about closeness."

Jaques said, "And will you, a man of your background, be married under a bush like a beggar? Go to a church. Have a good priest that can tell you what marriage is. This fellow will just join you like pieces of wood. Then one of you will change, like new wood that bends and warps."

Touchstone said to himself, "(Aside) I think it is better if he marries us badly. Then I will have a good reason to leave my wife later."

Jaques said, "Go with me, and let me advise you."

Touchstone said to Audrey, "Come, sweet Audrey. We must be married, or we will live wrongly. Farewell, good Master Oliver. Not, 'Oh sweet Oliver, Oh brave Oliver, Leave me not behind thee.' But, 'Go away, Begone, I say, I will not go to a wedding with thee.'"

Jaques, Touchstone, and Audrey left.

Sir Oliver Martext said, "It does not matter. None of those silly people will stop me from doing my job."

He left.

SCENE 4

In the forest, Rosalind and Celia were talking.

Rosalind said, "Never talk to me. I will weep." Rosalind's voice trembled a little when she spoke of Orlando.

Celia replied, "Do, please. But have the good sense to remember that tears do not suit a man."

Rosalind asked, "But do I not have cause to weep?"

Celia said, "As good cause as one would desire. Therefore weep."

Rosalind said, "His very hair color is deceitful."

Celia replied, "A bit browner than a false person's hair. Yes, his kisses are as false as that person."

Rosalind said, "Truly, his hair is of a good color."

Celia agreed, "An excellent color. Your chestnut was always the only color."

Rosalind said, "And his kissing is as pure as touching something holy."

Celia said, "He has lips like Diana's, the goddess of purity. A very pure nun could not kiss more purely. They are like ice." Celia thought Orlando's promises were like bubbles, pretty but quick to pop.

Rosalind asked, "But why did he swear he would come this morning, and he does not come?"

Celia answered, "No, certainly, there is no truth in him."

Rosalind asked, "Do you think so?"

Celia said, "Yes. I think he is not a thief or a horse-stealer. But for his truth in love, I think he is as empty as a covered cup or a nut eaten by a worm."

Rosalind asked, "Not true in love?"

Celia replied, "Yes, when he is in love. But I think he is not in love now."

Rosalind said, "You have heard him swear strongly he was."

Celia said, "'Was' is not 'is.' Besides, a lover's promise is no stronger than a bartender's word. Both confirm wrong bills. He is waiting here in the forest for the Duke, your father."

Rosalind said, "I met the Duke yesterday and talked much with him. He asked who my family was. I told him, as good as his. So he laughed and let me go. But why do we talk of fathers, when there is such a man as Orlando?"

Celia exclaimed, "Oh, that is a bold man! He writes bold poems. He speaks bold words. He makes bold promises and breaks them boldly. It is like a clumsy jouster who hits his opponent wrongly. He breaks his spear like a silly goose. But everything seems bold when young people do foolish things. Who comes here?"

Corin entered.

Corin said, "Mistress and master, you have often asked after the shepherd who complained of love. You saw him sitting by me on the grass. He was praising the proud, scornful shepherdess who was his mistress."

Celia asked, "Well, and what of him?"

Corin replied, "If you want to see a real show of true love's sadness and scorn's proud look, go a little way from here. I shall lead you, if you will watch it."

Rosalind said, "Oh, come, let us go. Seeing lovers helps those who are in love. Bring us to this sight. And you shall say I will be very involved in their situation."

They all left.

SCENE 5

In another part of the forest, Silvius and Phebe were talking.

Silvius pleaded, "Sweet Phebe, do not scorn me. Do not, Phebe. Say that you love me not. But do not say it in bitterness. Even the person who carries out punishments, whose heart is hardened by sad sights, asks for forgiveness first. Will you be harder than someone whose job involves sad endings?" Silvius followed Phebe like a little lamb follows its mother.

Rosalind, Celia, and Corin entered behind them, unseen.

Phebe said, "I would not be your punisher. I run from you, for I would not hurt you. You tell me my eyes can cause great harm. It is pretty, sure, and very likely. That eyes, which are the weakest and softest things, who close if even a tiny speck comes near, should be called cruel or harmful! Now I do frown on you with all my heart. And if my eyes can wound, now let them hurt you. Now pretend to faint. Why now fall down? Or if you cannot, oh, for shame, for shame! Do not lie and say my eyes are harmful! Now show the wound my eye has made in you. Scratch yourself with a pin, and a scar remains. If you lean on a reed, your hand keeps the mark for a moment. But now my eyes, which I have looked at you with, do not hurt you. Nor, I am sure, is there any force in eyes that can do hurt." Phebe's dark eyes flashed when she spoke to Silvius.

Silvius said, "Oh dear Phebe, if ever—and that may be soon—you fall in love with someone's pretty face, then you will know the unseen hurts that love can cause."

Phebe replied, "But until that time, do not come near me. And when that time comes, make fun of me, do not feel sorry for me. As until that time, I shall not feel sorry for you."

Rosalind stepped forward and asked, "And why, I ask you? Who was your mother, that you act so proud and mean to someone who is sad? What though you have no beauty—as, truly, I do not see much beauty in you. You are quite plain. Must you therefore be proud and pitiless? Why, what does this mean? Why do you look on me? I see nothing special in you. You look like an ordinary thing made by nature. Oh my!

I think she wants me to fall for her too! No, truly, proud mistress, do not hope for it. It is not your dark eyebrows, your black silky hair, your shiny eyes, or your creamy cheek that can make me admire you. You foolish shepherd, why do you follow her, like a misty wind bringing bad weather? You are a much better man than she is a woman. It is fools like you who make women think they are very pretty. It is not her mirror, but you, that tells her she is pretty. Because of you, she thinks she is more beautiful than she really is. But, mistress, know yourself. Down on your knees. And thank heaven, fasting, for a good man's love. For I must tell you friendly in your ear: Take a husband when you can. Not everyone will want you. Ask the man for mercy. Love him. Take his offer. Being plain is worse when you are also a mocker. So take her to you, shepherd. Fare you well."

Phebe said, "Sweet youth, I ask you, scold for a whole year. I would rather hear you scold than this man woo."

Rosalind said, "He has fallen in love with your plainness. And she will fall in love with my anger. If it is so, as fast as she answers you with frowning looks, I will answer her with bitter words. Why do you look so upon me?"

Phebe replied, "For no ill will I have for you."

Rosalind said, "I ask you, do not fall in love with me. For I am more untrustworthy than promises made when someone is tipsy. Besides, I like you not. If you want to know my house, it is at the group of olive trees nearby. Will you go, sister? Shepherd, try hard with her. Come, sister. Shepherdess, look on him better. And be not proud. Though all the world could see, no one would be as mistaken about looks as he is about you. Come, to our flock."

Rosalind, Celia, and Corin left.

Phebe said, "Dead Shepherd, now I find your strong saying true: 'Whoever loved that loved not at first sight?'"

Silvius said, "Sweet Phebe—"

Phebe interrupted, "Ha, what do you say, Silvius?"

Silvius pleaded, "Sweet Phebe, pity me."

Phebe replied, "Why, I am sorry for you, gentle Silvius."

Silvius said, "Wherever sadness is, help would be welcome. If you are sad for my love-sickness, by giving me love, both your sadness and my love-sickness would end."

Phebe said, "You have my friendship. Is that not neighborly?"

Silvius replied, "I would have you."

Phebe said, "Why, that would be wanting too much. Silvius, there was a time that I hated you. And it is not yet that I love you. But since you can talk of love so well, your company, which used to bother me, I will allow. And I will give you tasks to do. But do not look for more reward than your own happiness that you are employed."

Silvius said, "So holy and so perfect is my love. And I have so little hope of grace. I will think it a plentiful harvest to pick up the broken ears of grain after the man who reaps the main harvest. Give me a scattered smile now and then, and I will live on that."

Phebe asked, "Do you know the youth that spoke to me just now?"

Silvius answered, "Not very well, but I have met him often. And he has bought the cottage and the lands that the old peasant used to own."

Phebe said, "Do not think I love him, though I ask for him. He is just a grumpy boy, yet he talks well. But what do I care for words? Yet words do well when he that speaks them pleases those that hear. It is a pretty youth. Not very pretty. But, sure, he is proud, and yet his pride suits him. He will make a fine man. The best thing in him is his complexion. And faster than his tongue did cause offence, his eye did heal it up. He is not very tall, yet for his years he is tall. His leg is just so-so, and yet it is well. There was a pretty redness in his lip. A little deeper and more lively red than that mixed in his cheek. It was just the difference between a solid red and a mixed pink color. There are some women, Silvius, had they noticed him bit by bit as I did, would have nearly fallen in love with him.

But, for my part, I love him not nor hate him not. And yet I have more cause to hate him than to love him. For what right did he have to scold me? He said my eyes were black and my hair black. And, now I remember, he scorned me. I wonder why I did not answer back. But that is all one; just because I did not say anything then, does not mean I have forgotten. I will write to him a very taunting letter. And you shall carry it. Will you, Silvius?"

Silvius replied, "Phebe, with all my heart."

Phebe said, "I will write it right away. The matter is in my head and in my heart. I will be bitter with him and very brief. Go with me, Silvius."

They left.

ACT IV

SCENE 1

Jaques, Rosalind, and Celia walked into the forest. The air smelled fresh, like damp earth after a rain shower.

Jaques said, "Please, pretty young person, let me know you better."

Rosalind replied, "They say you are a sad fellow."

Jaques said, "I am. I like it more than laughing."

Rosalind told him, "People who are too much of either are not very nice. They show their faults to everyone. They are worse than people who drink too much."

Jaques asked, "Why, is it not good to be sad and say nothing?"

Rosalind answered, "Then it is good to be a wooden post."

Jaques explained, "My sadness is not like a student's, which is about wanting to be like others. It is not like a musician's, which is full of strange ideas. It is not like a courtier's, which is proud. It is not like a soldier's, which is wanting to achieve things. It is not like a lawyer's, which is clever. It is not like a lady's, which is fussy. It is not like a lover's, which is all of these. My sadness is my very own. It is made of many simple things. It comes from many things I have seen. Thinking about my travels wraps me in a funny kind of sadness."

Rosalind said, "A traveler! Truly, you have a big reason to be sad. I am afraid you sold your own lands to see other people's lands. Then, to have seen much and have nothing is like having rich eyes but poor hands."

Jaques replied, "Yes, I have gained my experience."

Rosalind said, "And your experience makes you sad. I would rather have a funny person to make me happy. That is better than experience that makes me sad. And to travel for it too!"

Orlando entered the forest.

Orlando called out, "Good day and happiness, dear Rosalind!"

Jaques said, "Well then, goodbye to you, if you are going to talk in fancy poetry." He then left.

Rosalind called after him, "Farewell, Mister Traveler! Make sure you talk with a funny accent. Wear strange clothes. Say bad things about your own country. Be unhappy with where you were born. Almost scold God for making you look the way you do. Or I will hardly think you have ever traveled far, perhaps in a boat in Venice! (She turned to Orlando.) Why, hello now, Orlando! Where have you been all this time? You call yourself a lover! If you play another trick like this on me, never come near me again."

Orlando said, "My fair Rosalind, I am only an hour late from my promise."

Rosalind replied, "Breaking an hour's promise in love! Someone who divides a minute into a thousand parts, and breaks even one tiny part of that minute in love matters, it might be said that Cupid has tapped him on the shoulder. But I promise you his heart is still whole."

Orlando pleaded, "Pardon me, dear Rosalind."

Rosalind said, "No, if you are so late, do not come near me anymore. I would rather be wooed by a snail."

Orlando asked, "By a snail?"

Rosalind said, "Yes, by a snail. Though he comes slowly, he carries his house on his head. That is a better home, I think, than you give a woman. Besides, he brings his future with him."

Orlando asked, "What is that?"

Rosalind explained, "Why, horns, which people like you often get because of your wives. But the snail comes ready for his fate. He avoids any bad talk about his wife."

Orlando stated, "Goodness does not make horns. And my Rosalind is good."

Rosalind said, "And I am your Rosalind (she said, pretending)."

Celia added, "It pleases him to call you so. But he has a Rosalind who looks better than you."

Rosalind said to Orlando, "Come, try to win my love. For now I am in a happy mood. I am likely to agree. What would you say to me now, if I were your very, very Rosalind?"

Orlando replied, "I would kiss you before I spoke."

Rosalind said, "No, you should speak first. When you run out of things to say, then you could kiss. Very good speakers, when they are stuck, they will spit. And for lovers who run out of things to say—goodness help us!—the cleanest thing to do is kiss."

Orlando asked, "What if the kiss is not allowed?"

Rosalind answered, "Then she makes you ask again. And then there are new things to talk about."

Orlando wondered, "Who could run out of things to say, when he is with his beloved lady?"

Rosalind said, "Well, you would, if I were your lady. Or I would think I was more honest than clever."

Orlando asked, "What, about my request?"

Rosalind replied, "Not out of your clothes, but out of your request. Am I not your Rosalind?"

Orlando said, "I feel some joy to say you are. Because I want to be talking about her."

Rosalind declared, "Well, as her, I say I will not have you."

Orlando said dramatically, "Then, as myself, I will pass away."

Rosalind replied, "No, truly, do not pass away like that. The poor world is almost six thousand years old. In all this time, no man has passed away in his own body, that is, for love. Troilus had his brains dashed out with a Greek club. Yet he did what he could to pass away before. He is one of the examples of love. Leander would have lived many good years, even if Hero had become a nun, if it had not been for a hot summer night. For, good young man, he only went to wash in the sea. He got a cramp and drowned. The foolish people of that time said it was 'Hero of Sestos.' But these are all lies. Men have passed away from time to time. Worms have eaten them. But not for love."

Orlando said, "I would not want my real Rosalind to think this way. I declare, her frown might make me very ill."

Rosalind said, "(Holding up her hand) By this hand, it will not harm a fly. But come, now I will be your Rosalind in a more agreeable mood. Ask me what you want. I will give it."

Orlando said, "Then love me, Rosalind."

Rosalind replied, "Yes, truly, I will. Fridays and Saturdays and all days."

Orlando asked, "And will you have me?"

Rosalind said, "Yes, and twenty like you."

Orlando asked, "What are you saying?"

Rosalind asked, "Are you not good?"

Orlando replied, "I hope so."

Rosalind said, "Why then, can one want too much of a good thing? Come, sister, you shall be the priest and marry us. Give me your hand, Orlando. What do you say, sister?"

Orlando urged, "Please, marry us."

Celia said, "I cannot say the words."

Rosalind instructed, "You must begin, 'Will you, Orlando—'"

Celia started, "Alright. Will you, Orlando, take this Rosalind as your wife?"

Orlando said, "I will."

Rosalind asked, "Yes, but when?"

Orlando replied, "Why now. As fast as she can marry us."

Rosalind said, "Then you must say 'I take you, Rosalind, for my wife.'"

Orlando repeated, "I take you, Rosalind, for my wife."

Rosalind said, "I might ask to see your permission. But I do take you, Orlando, for my husband. (She smiled.) There's a girl who goes before the priest! And certainly, a woman's thoughts run ahead of her actions."

Orlando agreed, "So do all thoughts. They have wings."

Rosalind asked, "Now tell me how long you would want her after you have her."

Orlando declared, "For ever and a day."

Rosalind corrected, "Say 'a day,' without the 'ever.' No, no, Orlando. Men are like April when they are trying to win love. They are like December when they are married. Maids are like May when they are maids. But the sky changes when they are wives. I will be more watchful of you than a pigeon over his hen. I will be noisier than a parrot before rain. I will want more new things than an ape. I will be more changeable in my wishes than a monkey. I will cry for nothing, like a statue in a fountain. I will do that when you want to be happy. I will laugh like a hyena. And that will be when you want to sleep."

Orlando asked, "But will my Rosalind do so?"

Rosalind replied, "By my life, she will do as I do."

Orlando said, "Oh, but she is wise."

Rosalind explained, "Or else she could not have the cleverness to do this. The wiser, the more mischievous. Try to lock up a woman's cleverness. It will get out at the window. Shut that, and it will get out at the key-hole. Stop that, it will fly with the smoke out of the chimney."

Orlando said, "A man who had a wife with such cleverness might say, 'Cleverness, where are you going?'"

Rosalind replied, "No, you might save that question. You could ask it when you find your wife's cleverness going to your neighbor's house."

Orlando asked, "And what clever excuse could there be for that?"

Rosalind said, "Well, to say she came to look for you there. You will never catch her without an answer. Unless you catch her without her tongue. Oh, that woman who cannot make her fault seem like her husband's doing, let her never nurse her own child. For she will raise it to be a fool!"

Orlando said, "For these two hours, Rosalind, I will leave you."

Rosalind cried, "Oh! Dear love, I cannot be without you for two hours."

Orlando explained, "I must join the Duke for dinner. By two o'clock I will be with you again."

Rosalind said, "Yes, go on your way. I knew what you would turn out to be. My friends told me so. I thought no less. That sweet-talking tongue of yours won me over. It is just one chance lost. And so, come, sadness! Two o'clock is your hour?"

Orlando confirmed, "Yes, sweet Rosalind."

Rosalind said, "By my truth, and in all seriousness, and so help me God, and by all pretty promises that are not dangerous, if you break one tiny bit of your promise, or come one minute after your hour, I will think you are the most terrible promise-breaker. You would be the most empty lover. You would be the most unworthy of her you call Rosalind. You could be chosen from the whole group of unfaithful people.

Therefore, be careful of my judgment and keep your promise."

Orlando promised, "With no less seriousness than if you were indeed my Rosalind. So, goodbye." He left.

Rosalind said, "Well, Time is the old judge that questions all such rule-breakers. Let Time decide. Goodbye."

Celia said, "You have simply spoken badly of our gender in your love-talk. We should pull your shirt and pants over your head. We should show the world what the bird has done to her own nest."

Rosalind cried, "Oh cousin, cousin, cousin, my pretty little cousin! If only you knew how deeply I am in love! But it cannot be measured. My love has an unknown bottom, like a deep bay in the sea."

Celia replied, "Or rather, it has no bottom. As fast as you pour love in, it runs out."

Rosalind said, "No, that same naughty child of Venus, who was created by thought, imagined from bad moods, and born of madness, that blind naughty boy who tricks every-one's eyes because his own cannot see, let him be the judge of how deep I am in love. I will tell you, Aliena, I cannot be out of Orlando's sight. I will go find a shady spot and sigh until he comes."

Celia said, "And I will sleep." They both left.

SCENE 2

Jaques, some Lords, and Foresters entered another part of the forest. The birds chirped loudly in the trees.

Jaques asked, "Which one is he that killed the deer?"

A Lord replied, "Sir, it was I."

Jaques said, "Let's present him to the Duke, like a Roman hero. It would be good to set the deer's horns upon his head, as a sign of victory. Do you have a song, forester, for this?"

A Forester answered, "Yes, sir."

Jaques said, "Sing it. It does not matter if it is in tune, as long as it makes enough noise."

The Forester sang:

"What shall he have that killed the deer?

His leather skin and horns to wear.

Then sing him home."

The others joined in for the chorus: "Do not be ashamed to wear the horn. It was a special mark before you were born. Your grandfather wore it. And your father carried it. The horn, the horn, the strong horn, is not a thing to laugh at."

They all left, still singing.

SCENE 3

Rosalind and Celia entered the forest. The sun was high, making patterns on the ground.

Rosalind asked, "What do you say now? Is it not past two o'clock? And Orlando is very much not here!"

Celia replied, "I promise you, with pure love and a troubled brain, he has taken his bow and arrows. He has gone off to sleep. Look, who comes here."

Silvius entered.

Silvius said, "My message is to you, fair young person. My gentle Phebe asked me to give you this. (He held out a letter.) I do not know what it says. But, as I guess by her stern face and cross way she acted while writing it, it has an angry message. Pardon me. I am only an innocent messenger."

Rosalind took the letter. "Patience herself would be surprised by this letter. She would act like a tough person. If I can bear this, I can bear anything. She says I am not pretty. She says I lack manners. She calls me proud. She says she could not love me, even if men were as rare as a special bird called a phoenix. Goodness me! Her love is not the rabbit I am hunting. Why does she write this to me? Well, shepherd, well, this is a letter you wrote yourself."

Silvius protested, "No, I promise, I do not know what it says. Phebe wrote it."

Rosalind said, "Come, come, you are a fool. You have become completely lost in love. I saw her hand. She has a leathery hand. A tan-colored hand. I really thought her old gloves were on, but it was her hands. She has a hardworking woman's hand. But that does not matter. I say she never made up this letter. This is a man's idea and his hand-writing."

Silvius insisted, "Surely, it is hers."

Rosalind said, "Why, it is a rough and cruel style. A style for challengers. Why, she challenges me, like an enemy. A woman's gentle brain could not produce such a hugely rude idea. Such dark words, darker in their meaning than they look. Will you hear the letter?"

Silvius replied, "If you please. For I have never heard it yet. Yet I have heard too much of Phebe's cruelty."

Rosalind said, "She is 'Phebe-ing' me. Mark how the mean person writes. (She began to read.)

> *'Are you a god turned into a shepherd,*
> *That a maiden's heart has been made to feel*
> > *strongly?'*

Can a woman complain like this?"

Silvius asked, "Do you call this complaining?"

Rosalind read on:

> *'"Why, putting your god-like nature aside,*
> *Do you fight with a woman's heart?'*
> *Did you ever hear such complaining?*
> *'While men's eyes tried to win me,*
> *That could do no harm to me.'*
> *(Rosalind commented.) Meaning I am like a*
> > *beast.*
> *'If the scorn from your bright eyes*
> *Has power to create such love in mine,*
> *Oh dear, in me what strange effect*
> *Would they create if they looked kindly!*
> *While you scolded me, I did love;*

How then might your prayers move me!

He that brings this love letter to you

Little knows about this love in me.

And by him, make up your mind;

Whether your youth and kindness

Will take the faithful offer

Of me and all that I can give;

Or else by him deny my love,

And then I'll think of how to become very sad.'"

Silvius asked, "Do you call this scolding?"

Celia said softly, "Alas, poor shepherd!"

Rosalind asked Silvius, "Do you pity him? No, he deserves no pity. Will you love such a woman? What, to make you like an instrument and play untrue songs on you! It is not to be tolerated! Well, go your way to her. For I see love has made you a tame snake. Say this to her: that if she loves me, I order her to love you. If she will not, I will never have her unless you ask for her. If you are a true lover, go now, and not a word. For here comes more company."

Silvius left sadly. Oliver entered.

Oliver said, "Good morning, fair ones. Please, if you know, where in the edges of this forest stands a sheep-pen fenced with olive trees?"

Celia replied, "West of this place, down in the nearby valley. The row of willow branches by the softly flowing stream, left on your right hand, will bring you to the place. But at this hour the house is empty. There is no one inside."

Oliver said, "If an eye may learn from a tongue, then I should know you by description. Such clothes and such ages: 'The boy is fair, with a girl's looks, and carries himself like a grown-up sister. The woman is shorter and darker than her brother.' Are you not the owner of the house I asked for?"

Celia answered, "It is no boast, since you asked, to say we are."

Oliver said, "Orlando sends his greetings to you both. And to that young person he calls his Rosalind, he sends this bloody handkerchief. Are you he?"

Rosalind confirmed, "I am. What must we understand by this?"

Oliver replied, "Some of my shame. If you will learn from me what man I am, and how, and why, and where this handkerchief was stained."

Celia urged, "Please, tell it."

Oliver began, "When young Orlando last parted from you, he promised to return within an hour. While walking through the forest, thinking deeply of sweet and bitter things, look what happened! He glanced aside. And see what he saw! Under an oak tree, whose branches were mossy with age and its top bare, a poor, ragged man, overgrown with hair, lay sleeping on his back. Around his neck, a green and gold snake had wrapped itself. Its head moved quickly, threatening to go into the man's open mouth. But suddenly, seeing Orlando, it uncoiled itself. It slipped away into a bush with quick slides. Under that bush's shade, a lioness, very thin and hungry, lay crouching. Her head was on the ground, watching like a cat for when the sleeping man should stir. For it is the royal nature of that beast to attack nothing that seems not alive. Seeing this, Orlando approached the man. He found it was his brother, his older brother."

Celia exclaimed, "Oh, I have heard him speak of that same brother! And he described him as the most unnatural man that lived."

Oliver said, "And well he might say so. For I know well I was unnatural."

Rosalind asked urgently, "But, about Orlando! Did he leave him there, food for the hungry lioness?"

Oliver continued, "Twice he turned his back and planned to do so. But kindness, always nobler than revenge, and family feeling, stronger than his reason to be angry, made him fight the lioness. She quickly fell before him. During that struggle, I awoke from my miserable sleep."

Celia asked, "Are you his brother?"

Rosalind asked, "Were you the one he rescued?"

Celia pressed, "Was it you that so often tried to harm him?"

Oliver confessed, "'It was I. But it is not I now. I am not ashamed to tell you what I was. Since my change of heart tastes so sweet, being the person I am now."

Rosalind asked, "But, about the bloody handkerchief?"

Oliver said, "Soon. When, from first to last between us two, tears had kindly washed our stories, like how I came into that wild place. In short, he led me to the gentle Duke. The Duke gave me fresh clothes and food. He put me in my brother's care. My brother led me at once to his cave. There he took off his own shirt. Here upon his arm, the lioness had torn some flesh away. It had been bleeding all this while. And now he fainted. And cried out, while fainting, for Rosalind. Briefly, I helped him recover. I bound up his wound. And after a short time, being strong at heart, he sent me here, stranger though I am. He sent me to tell this story, so that you might excuse his broken promise. And to give this handkerchief, stained with his blood, to the shepherd youth that he playfully calls his Rosalind."

Rosalind suddenly swayed, her eyes closing.

Celia cried out, "Why, how now, Ganymede! Sweet Ganymede!"

Oliver remarked, "Many will feel faint when they look on blood."

Celia said, "There is more to it. Cousin Ganymede!"

Oliver said, "Look, he is recovering."

Rosalind whispered, "I wish I were at home."

Celia said, "We will lead you there. (To Oliver) Please, will you take him by the arm?"

Oliver said kindly, "Be of good cheer, youth. You are a man! You lack a man's courage."

Rosalind confessed, "I do so, I admit it. Ah, sir, a person would think this was well pretended! Please, tell your brother how well I pretended. Heigh-ho!"

Oliver said, "This was not pretended. There is too much proof in your pale face that it was a real feeling."

Rosalind insisted, "Pretended, I assure you."

Oliver replied, "Well then, take a good heart and pretend to be a man."

Rosalind said, "So I do. But, in truth, I should have been a woman by right."

Celia urged, "Come, you look paler and paler. Please, let's go towards home. Good sir, go with us."

Oliver agreed, "That I will. For I must carry an answer back about how you excuse my brother, Rosalind."

Rosalind said, "I shall think of something. But, please, praise my pretending to him. Will you go?"

They all left together.

ACT V

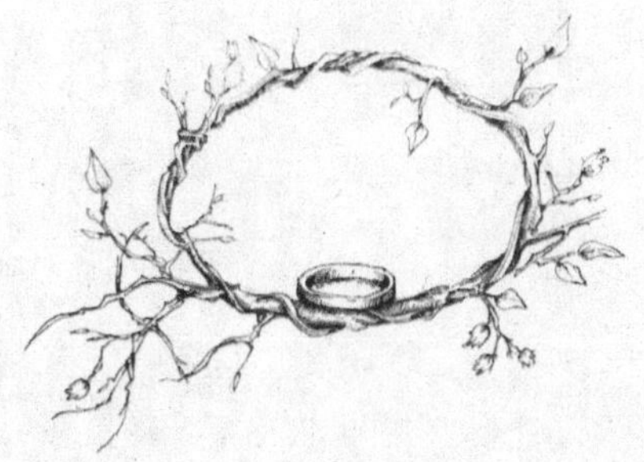

SCENE I

Touchstone and Audrey walked into the forest.

Touchstone said, "We will find a time, Audrey. Be patient, gentle Audrey."

Audrey replied, "Truly, the priest was good enough. It does not matter what the old gentleman said."

Touchstone said, "He was a very naughty Sir Oliver, Audrey. A very bad Martext. But Audrey, a young man here in the forest says you belong to him."

Audrey said, "Yes, I know who it is. He has no claim on me at all. Here comes the man you mean."

William entered. The leaves crunched softly under his feet.

Touchstone said, "It is like food and drink to me to see a silly fellow. Truly, we who are clever have much to explain. We will make fun; we cannot stop ourselves." He always liked to show how smart he was.

William said, "Good evening, Audrey."

Audrey replied, "Good evening to you, William."

William said, "And good evening to you, sir."

Touchstone said, "Good evening, gentle friend. Cover your head, cover your head. No, please, be covered. How old are you, friend?"

William answered, "Twenty-five, sir."

Touchstone said, "A good age. Is your name William?"

William replied, "William, sir."

Touchstone said, "A nice name. Were you born here in the forest?"

William answered, "Yes, sir, I thank God."

Touchstone said, "'Thank God.' A good answer. Are you rich?"

William replied, "Truly, sir, so-so."

Touchstone said, "'So-so' is good, very good, very excellent good. And yet it is not. It is just so-so. Are you wise?"

William answered, "Yes, sir, I am quite clever."

Touchstone said, "Why, you say it well. I remember a saying: 'The fool thinks he is wise. But the wise man knows he is a fool.' A wise man from long ago, when he wanted to eat a grape, would open his lips when he put it in his mouth. This means grapes were made to eat and lips to open. Do you love this young woman?"

William replied, "I do, sir."

Touchstone said, "Give me your hand. Are you learned?"

William answered, "No, sir."

Touchstone said, "Then learn this from me. To have is to have. It is a way of speaking. Drink poured from a cup into a glass fills one and empties the other. All writers agree that 'ipse' means 'he.' Now, you are not 'ipse,' for I am he."

William asked, "Which he, sir?"

Touchstone replied, "He, sir, that must marry this woman. Therefore, you silly fellow, leave. That means go away from the company of this female. That means this woman. All together it means: leave the company of this female. Or, silly fellow, you will be in trouble. Or, so you understand better, you will be gone. I mean I will make you go away. I have many ways to make you leave. So tremble and go."

Audrey said, "Do it, good William."

William said, "May God keep you happy, sir."

William left.

Corin entered.

Corin said, "Our master and mistress are looking for you. Come, away, away!"

Touchstone said, "Let's go, Audrey! Let's go, Audrey! I am coming, I am coming."

They all left.

SCENE 2

Orlando and Oliver were in the forest.

Orlando asked, "Is it possible that you like her after knowing her so little? That just seeing her made you love her? And loving her, you asked her to marry you? And asking, she agreed? And will you keep on wanting to be with her?"

Oliver replied, "Do not question how fast it happened. Or that she is not rich, or that we just met. Or my sudden asking, or her sudden agreement. But say with me, I love Aliena. Say with her that she loves me. Agree with both of us that we may be together. It will be good for you. I will give you my father's house. And all the money that was old Sir Rowland's. I will live and die a shepherd here."

Orlando said, "You have my agreement. Let your wedding be tomorrow. I will invite the Duke Senior and all his happy followers there. You go and prepare Aliena. For look, here comes my Rosalind."

Rosalind entered. Her green forest clothes looked bright.

Rosalind said, "God save you, brother."

Oliver replied, "And you, fair sister."

Oliver left.

Rosalind said, "Oh, my dear Orlando, it makes me sad to see you wear your heart in a scarf!"

Orlando said, "It is my arm."

Rosalind said, "I thought your heart had been wounded by the claws of a lion."

Orlando replied, "It is wounded, but by the eyes of a lady."

Rosalind asked, "Did your brother tell you how I pretended to faint when he showed me your handkerchief?"

Orlando answered, "Yes, and greater wonders than that."

Rosalind said, "Oh, I know what you mean. No, it is true. Nothing was ever so sudden. Except for the fight of two rams. Or Caesar's proud boast of 'I came, I saw, I conquered.' Your brother and my sister met. Then they looked. Then they loved. Then they sighed. Then they asked each other why. Then they knew the reason. Then they found the answer. In these steps they have made stairs to marriage. They will climb them right away. Or they will be impatient before marriage. They are very much in love. They will be together. Nothing can part them." It was quite a fast romance, like in a storybook!

Orlando said, "They shall be married tomorrow. I will ask the Duke Senior to the wedding. But, oh, how sad it is to see happiness through another man's eyes! I will be very sad tomorrow. I will think how happy my brother is. He has what he wishes for."

Rosalind asked, "Why then, tomorrow can I not help you get Rosalind?"

Orlando replied, "I can live no longer by just thinking."

Rosalind said, "I will not tire you then with silly talk. Know this from me, for I speak seriously now. I know you are a gentleman of good understanding. I do not say this so you think well of my knowledge. I say I know you are. I do not try for more respect than what might make you believe me. This is to do yourself good, not to praise me. Believe then, if you please, that I can do strange things. Since I was three years old, I have talked with a magician. He was very skilled in his art but not bad. If you love Rosalind as much as you show, when your brother marries Aliena, you shall marry her. I know what troubles she has. It is not impossible for me to bring her before your eyes tomorrow. She will be herself and without any danger, if it is not difficult for you."

Orlando asked, "Are you speaking seriously?"

Rosalind replied, "By my life, I am. I value my life greatly, though I say I am a magician. Therefore, put on your best clothes. Invite your friends. For if you will be married tomorrow, you shall. And to Rosalind, if you will."

Silvius and Phebe entered.

Rosalind said, "Look, here comes someone who loves me and someone she loves."

Phebe said, "Youth, you have been very unkind to me. You showed the letter that I wrote to you."

Rosalind replied, "I do not care if I have. It is my plan to seem mean and unkind to you. You are followed by a faithful shepherd. Look at him, love him; he adores you."

Phebe said, "Good shepherd, tell this youth what it is to love."

Silvius said, "It is to be all made of sighs and tears. And so am I for Phebe."

Phebe said, "And I for Ganymede."

Orlando said, "And I for Rosalind."

Rosalind said, "And I for no woman."

Silvius said, "It is to be all made of faith and service. And so am I for Phebe."

Phebe said, "And I for Ganymede."

Orlando said, "And I for Rosalind."

Rosalind said, "And I for no woman."

Silvius said, "It is to be all made of imagination. All made of strong feeling and all made of wishes. All adoration, duty, and respect. All humbleness, all patience and impatience. All purity, all trial, all respect. And so am I for Phebe."

Phebe said, "And so am I for Ganymede."

Orlando said, "And so am I for Rosalind."

Rosalind said, "And so am I for no woman."

Phebe asked, "(To Rosalind) If this is so, why blame me for loving you?"

Silvius asked, "(To Phebe) If this is so, why blame me for loving you?"

Orlando asked, "(To Rosalind) If this is so, why blame me for loving you?"

Rosalind asked, "Who are you speaking to, 'Why blame you me to love you?'"

Orlando replied, "To her that is not here, and does not hear."

Rosalind said, "Please, no more of this. It is like the howling of Irish wolves against the moon. (To Silvius) I will help you, if I can. (To Phebe) I would love you, if I could. Tomorrow, meet me all together. (To Phebe) I will marry you, if I ever marry a woman. And I will be married tomorrow. (To Orlando) I will make you happy, if I ever made a man happy. And you shall be married tomorrow. (To Silvius) I will make you content, if what pleases you makes you content. And you shall be married tomorrow. (To Orlando) As you love Rosalind, meet. (To Silvius) As you love Phebe, meet. And as I love no woman, I will meet. So goodbye. I have left you instructions."

Silvius said, "I will not fail, if I live."

Phebe said, "Nor I."

Orlando said, "Nor I."

They all left.

SCENE 3

Touchstone and Audrey were in the forest.

Touchstone said, "Tomorrow is the joyful day, Audrey. Tomorrow we will be married."

Audrey replied, "I want it with all my heart. And I hope it is not a bad wish to want to be a married woman. Here come two of the banished Duke Senior's pages."

Two Pages entered. Their shoes made little scuffing sounds on the path.

First Page said, "Well met, honest gentleman."

Touchstone replied, "Truly, well met. Come, sit, sit, and a song."

Second Page said, "We are ready for you. Sit in the middle."

First Page asked, "Shall we start right away? Without coughing or spitting or saying we are hoarse? Those are just excuses for a bad voice."

Second Page said, "Yes, indeed! And both in tune, like two gypsies on a horse."

They sang a song:

> *"It was a lover and his sweetheart,*
> *With a hey, and a ho, and a hey nonino,*
> *That over the green corn-field did pass*
> *In the springtime, the only pretty ring time,*
> *When birds do sing, hey ding a ding, ding:*
> *Sweet lovers love the spring.*
> *Between the fields of rye,*
> *With a hey, and a ho, and a hey nonino,*
> *These pretty country folks would lie,*
> *In springtime, etc.*
> *This carol they began that hour,*
> *With a hey, and a ho, and a hey nonino,*
> *How that a life was but a flower*
> *In springtime, etc.*
> *And therefore take the present time,*
> *With a hey, and a ho, and a hey nonino;*
> *For love is best in its prime*
> *In springtime, etc."*

Even if Touchstone didn't like it, songs could still be fun to hear.

Touchstone said, "Truly, young gentlemen, though there was no great meaning in the song, the tune was very off-key."

First Page said, "You are mistaken, sir. We kept time, we did not lose our time."

Touchstone replied, "Truly, yes. I count it but time lost to hear such a foolish song. Goodbye to you. And may your voices get better! Come, Audrey."

They left.

SCENE 4

Duke Senior, Amiens, Jaques, Orlando, Oliver, and Celia were in the forest.

Duke Senior asked, "Do you believe, Orlando, that the boy can do all this that he has promised?"

Orlando replied, "Sometimes I do believe, and sometimes I do not. Like those who fear what they hope for, and know they fear."

Rosalind, Silvius, and Phebe entered.

Rosalind said, "Patience once more, while our agreement is stated. (To Duke Senior) You say, if I bring in your Rosalind, you will give her to Orlando here?"

Duke Senior replied, "That I would, if I had kingdoms to give with her."

Rosalind said, "(To Orlando) And you say, you will have her, when I bring her?"

Orlando replied, "That I would, if I were king of all kingdoms."

Rosalind said, "(To Phebe) You say, you will marry me, if I am willing?"

Phebe replied, "That I will, even if I die the hour after."

Rosalind said, "But if you refuse to marry me, you will give yourself to this most faithful shepherd?"

Phebe replied, "So is the bargain."

Rosalind said, "(To Silvius) You say, that you will have Phebe, if she will?"

Silvius replied, "Though to have her and death were both one thing."

Rosalind said, "I have promised to make all this clear. Keep your word, O Duke Senior, to give your daughter. You yours, Orlando, to receive his daughter. Keep your word, Phebe, that you will marry me. Or else, refusing me, to wed this shepherd. Keep your word, Silvius, that you will marry her if she refuses me. And from here I go, to make these doubts all clear."

Rosalind and Celia left.

Duke Senior said, "I do remember in this shepherd boy some clear signs of my daughter's looks."

Orlando said, "My lord, the first time I ever saw him, I thought he was a brother to your daughter. But, my good lord, this boy was born in the forest. He has been taught the basics of many difficult studies by his uncle. He says his uncle is a great magician, hidden in this forest."

Touchstone and Audrey entered.

Jaques said, "There is, surely, another big flood coming. And these couples are coming to the ark. Here comes a pair of very strange animals, which in all languages are called fools."

Touchstone said, "Hello and greeting to you all!"

Jaques said, "Good my lord, welcome him. This is the funny-minded gentleman I have so often met in the forest. He swears he has been a courtier."

Touchstone said, "If any man doubts that, let him test me. I have danced a formal dance. I have flattered a lady. I have been clever with my friend, smooth with my enemy. I have caused three tailors to lose business. I have had four quarrels, and almost fought one."

Jaques asked, "And how was that settled?"

Touchstone replied, "Truly, we met. We found the quarrel was about the seventh cause."

Jaques asked, "How seventh cause? Good my lord, like this fellow."

Duke Senior said, "I like him very well."

Touchstone said, "God reward you, sir. I wish the same for you. I push in here, sir, among the rest of the country couples. To swear and to unswear. According as marriage ties and feelings break. A poor young woman, sir. An unattractive thing, sir, but my own. A poor wish of mine, sir, to take what no man else will. Rich honesty lives like a stingy person, sir, in a poor house. Like your pearl in your dirty oyster."

Duke Senior said, "By my faith, he is very quick and speaks wisely."

Touchstone said, "According to the fool's arrow, sir, and such sweet troubles."

Jaques said, "But, for the seventh cause. How did you find the quarrel on the seventh cause?"

Touchstone replied, "Upon a lie seven times removed. (To Audrey) Hold your body more properly, Audrey. Like this, sir. I did not like the cut of a certain courtier's beard. He sent me word, if I said his beard was not cut well, he thought it was. This is called the Polite Answer. If I sent him word again 'it was not well cut,' he would send me word, he cut it to please himself. This is called the Clever Quip. If again 'it was not well cut,' he insulted my judgment. This is called the Rude Reply. If again 'it was not well cut,' he would answer, I did not speak true. This is called the Brave Correction. If again 'it was not well cut,' he would say I lied. This is called the Argumentative Check. And so to the Indirect Lie and the Direct Lie."

Jaques asked, "And how often did you say his beard was not well cut?"

Touchstone replied, "I dared go no further than the Indirect Lie. Nor dared he give me the Direct Lie. And so we drew swords and parted."

Jaques asked, "Can you name in order now the steps of the lie?"

Touchstone said, "Oh sir, we quarrel by the book, like you have books for good manners. I will name you the steps. The first, the Polite Answer. The second, the Clever Quip. The third, the Rude Reply. The fourth, the Brave Correction. The fifth, the Argumentative Check. The sixth, the Lie with Circumstance. The seventh, the Direct Lie. All these you may avoid but the Direct Lie. And you may avoid that too, with an 'If.' I knew when seven judges could not settle a quarrel. But when the people met themselves, one of them thought of an 'If.' As, 'If you said so, then I said so.' And they shook hands and swore to be like brothers. Your 'If' is the only peace-maker. Much good in 'If.'"

Jaques asked, "Is not this a rare fellow, my lord? He is as good at anything and yet a fool."

Duke Senior said, "He uses his foolishness like a disguise. And under that, he shows his cleverness."

Hymen, Rosalind, and Celia entered. Soft music played, like a gentle breeze.

Hymen said, "Then there is joy in heaven, when earthly things made even, come together. Good Duke Senior, receive your daughter. Hymen from heaven brought her. Yes, brought her here. So that you might join her hand with his whose heart is in his chest."

Rosalind said, "(To Duke Senior) To you I give myself, for I am yours. (To Orlando) To you I give myself, for I am yours."

Duke Senior said, "If what I see is true, you are my daughter."

Orlando said, "If what I see is true, you are my Rosalind."

Phebe said, "If sight and shape are true, why then, my love, goodbye!"

Rosalind said, "(To Duke Senior) I will have no father, if you are not he. (To Orlando) I will have no husband, if you are not he. (To Phebe) Nor ever wed a woman, if you are not she."

Hymen said, "Peace, ho! I stop confusion. It is I who must make an end of these most strange events. Here are eight that must take hands to join in Hymen's groups, if truth holds true. (To Orlando and Rosalind) You two no trouble shall part. (To Oliver and Celia) You two are heart in heart. (To Phebe) You to his love must agree, or have a woman as your partner. (To Touchstone and Audrey) You and you are sure together, as winter is to bad weather. While we sing a wedding song, talk among yourselves. So that wonder may lessen, how we met, and these things finish."

They sang a song:

"Wedding is great Juno's crown:

Oh blessed bond of table and bed!

It is Hymen who fills every town;

High wedlock then be honored:

Honor, high honor and fame,

To Hymen, helper of every town!"

Duke Senior said, "Oh my dear niece, welcome you are to me! Even daughter, welcome, in no less amount."

Phebe said, "(To Silvius) I will not go back on my word, now you are mine. Your faith makes my heart choose you."

Jaques de Boys entered.

Jaques de Boys said, "Let me speak for a word or two. I am the second son of old Sir Rowland. I bring this news to this fine group. Duke Frederick heard how every day men of great worth came to this forest. He gathered a mighty army. They were on foot, led by himself, planning to take his brother here and harm him. And to the edge of this wild wood he came. There he met an old religious man. After some talk with him, he changed his mind. Both about his plan and about the world. He is giving his crown to his banished brother. And all their lands are restored to them again that were exiled with him. I promise my life this is true."

Duke Senior said, "Welcome, young man. You offer good things to your brothers' wedding. To one, his lands that were kept from him. And to the other, a land itself, a powerful dukedom. First, in this forest, let us finish those things that were well begun and well started here. And after, every one of this happy group that has faced hard days and nights with us shall share the good of our returned fortune. According to their rank. Meantime, forget this new honor and join in our country fun. Play, music! And you, brides and bridegrooms all, with much joy, begin to dance." Everyone felt happy, like sunshine after a rainy day.

Jaques said, "Sir, if you please. If I heard you right, the Duke Frederick has chosen a religious life? And left behind the fancy court?"

Jaques de Boys replied, "He has."

Jaques said, "To him I will go. From these people who have changed their lives, there is much to be heard and learned. (To Duke Senior) To you, I leave your former honor. Your patience and your goodness well deserve it. (To Orlando) To you, a love that your true faith earns. (To Oliver) To you, your land and love and great friends. (To Silvius) To you, a long and well-deserved marriage. (To Touchstone) And you to arguing. For your loving journey is supplied for only two months. So, to your pleasures. I am for other things than dancing."

Duke Senior said, "Stay, Jaques, stay."

Jaques replied, "To see no fun, I will stay to know what you want at your empty cave."

Jaques left.

Duke Senior said, "Go on, go on. We will þegin these cere-monies. As we trust they will end, in true delights."

They had a dance.

EPILOGUE

Rosalind stepped forward.

Rosalind said, "It is not usual to see the lady give the epilogue. But it is no more strange than to see the lord give the prologue. If it is true that good wine needs no sign, it is true that a good play needs no epilogue. Yet for good wine they do use good signs. And good plays are better with the help of good epilogues. What a spot I am in then! I am not a good epilogue. Nor can I ask you nicely for a good play. I am not dressed like a beggar, so to beg will not suit me. My way is to ask you earnestly. And I will begin with the women. I ask you, O women, for the love you have for men, to like as much of this play as pleases you. And I ask you, O men, for the love you have for women—as I see by your smiles, none of you dislikes them—that between you and the women the play may please. If I were truly a woman, I would give a friendly greeting to as many of you as had beards that pleased me, looks that I liked, and breath that I did not mind. And, I am sure, as many as have good beards or good faces or sweet breaths will, for my kind offer, when I curtsy, bid me farewell."

They all left.

THE WHIMS AND WONDERS OF "AS YOU LIKE IT"

Once upon a time, in a play called "As You Like It," William Shakespeare tells a story full of fun, forests, and some very mixed-up love stories. Imagine a world where princesses pretend to be someone else, where forests are magical places that can change how you see the world, and where everyone ends up happy.

A Forest Full of Surprises: The story takes us to the Forest of Arden, a place where the usual rules don't apply. People who are usually very serious find themselves doing silly things, and those who are sad find reasons to smile. It's like the forest has a special power to make everyone forget their problems and just enjoy life.

Rosalind's Clever Disguise: Imagine having to dress up as someone else to stay safe, but also to teach your best friend how to woo the girl of his dreams—who is actually you! That's exactly what Rosalind does, and it leads to all sorts of funny situations. She shows us that sometimes, you have to be a little bit sneaky to help everyone find their happy ending.

Love is Everywhere: In "As You Like It," love pops up in the most unexpected places. People fall in love at first sight, argue then make up, and sometimes they don't even realize they're in love until the very end. It's a wild ride through the ups and downs of love, with lots of laughter along the way.

The Wise Fool: There's a character in the play who might seem silly at first, but he's actually super smart. He makes jokes, but also makes you think. It's like he knows a secret about life and love that he's trying to share, if only everyone would listen.

Happily Ever After: In the end, "As You Like It" teaches us that forgiveness and saying sorry can fix even the biggest messes. The magical forest helps everyone find their best selves and leads them to a happy ending, with lots of laughter, love, and new friendships.

Why This Story Rocks: Shakespeare might have written this story a long time ago, but it's still super fun to read and watch because it's all about adventure, dressing up, falling in silly love, and finding out who you really are—all in a magical forest that feels like a fairy tale.

So, "As You Like It" is a play where the magic of the forest teaches everyone about love, life, and laughter, proving that sometimes, you need a little bit of silliness to make everything right in the world.

THE LIFE OF WILLIAM SHAKESPEARE

Step back in time with us as we discover the exciting life of **William Shakespeare**—a storyteller whose magnificent tales have been told and retold for hundreds of years. Fasten your seatbelts for some amazing facts about the Bard of Avon!

Birthday Mystery: Believe it or not, we don't know exactly when Shakespeare was born. Historians guess it was around April 23, 1564, but that's all because of the date of his baptism. How curious that such a famous person has a birthday shrouded in mystery!

. . .

School Days: Young Shakespeare attended the King's New School in his hometown, where he learned important subjects like Latin, Greek, history, and poetry—all without the gadgets and technology students have today.

Word Wizard: Shakespeare had a way with words, inventing over 1,700 of them! Imagine, every time you say "bedroom" or "excitement," you're using words that Shakespeare introduced to the English language.

Globe Trotter - But Not Really: The Globe Theatre is where Shakespeare's masterpieces were first performed—not a globe you can spin, but a large, round, open-air theater where audiences marveled under the sky.

Super-sized Works: Our dear Bard wrote 37 plays and 154 sonnets. That's a lot of storytelling! If you wrote a poem every week of the year, you'd still be short of Shakespeare's sonnet count.

Nicknamed "The Bard": Shakespeare is often referred to as "The Bard of Avon." 'Bard' means poet, and indeed, Shakespeare was a master poet from the town of Stratford-upon-Avon.

Lovey-Dovey Lines: Shakespeare's words about love are so beautiful that they are still read at weddings and shared between sweethearts today. And if you've heard the phrase "to be or not to be," you're quoting one of his most famous lines!

Queen for a Fan: Queen Elizabeth I loved the theater, and Shakespeare's plays were some of her most enjoyed performances. It was quite the honor for Shakespeare to entertain her majesty with his work.

Shakespeare's Secret Code: Some folks believe that Shakespeare tucked away secret codes within his plays—making each performance not just a show, but also a puzzle full of hidden meanings.

Goodnight, Sweet Prince: At age 52, in the year 1616, Shakespeare took his final bow. His presence may be missed, but his stories live on, continuing to inspire, entertain, and provoke thought across the globe.

. . .

So there you have it—a little peek into the life of the man who has kept us company through his words for over four centuries. Open the pages of his stories, and let William Shakespeare's plays transport you to a world where imagination knows no bounds. Happy reading!

SHAKESPEARE FOR KIDS – OTHER BOOKS IN THE SERIES

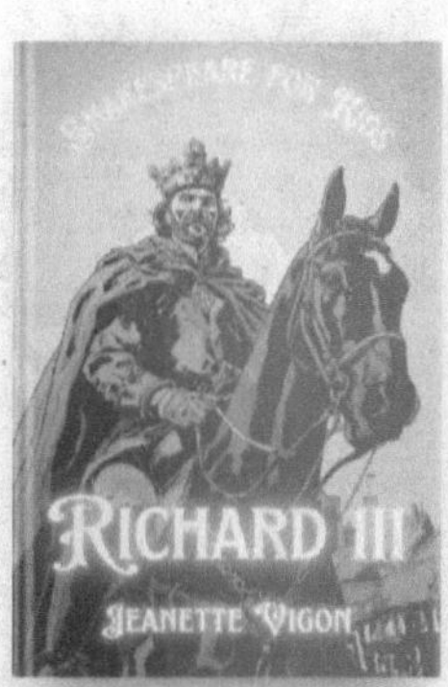

SHAKESPEARE FOR KIDS
MUCH ADO ABOUT NOTHING
JEANETTE VIGON

SHAKESPEARE FOR KIDS
THE COMEDY OF ERRORS
JEANETTE VIGON

SHAKESPEARE FOR KIDS
AS YOU LIKE IT
JEANETTE VIGON

SHAKESPEARE FOR KIDS
THE MERCHANT OF VENICE
JEANETTE VIGON

SHAKESPEARE FOR KIDS
THE TEMPEST
JEANETTE VIGON

SHAKESPEARE FOR KIDS
KING LEAR
JEANETTE VIGON

SHAKESPEARE FOR KIDS
A MIDSUMMER NIGHT'S DREAM
JEANETTE VIGON

SHAKESPEARE FOR KIDS
JULIUS CAESAR
JEANETTE VIGON

SHAKESPEARE FOR KIDS
HAMLET
JEANETTE VIGON

You can find the rest of the books in the series here:
https://amzn.to/3wLXpTC

www.ingramcontent.com/pod-product-compliance
Lightning Source LLC
Chambersburg PA
CBHW012018110726
47994CB00009B/3208